N. L. FOX

"He" Says I'm Beautiful

TATE PUBLISHING
AND ENTERPRISES, LLC

Scripture quotations marked (AMP) are taken from the *Amplified Bible*, Copyright © 1954, 1958, 1962, 1964, 1965, 1987 by The Lockman Foundation. Used by permission.

Scripture quotations marked (MSG) are taken from *The Message*. Copyright © 1993, 1994, 1995, 1996, 2000, 2001, 2002. Used by permission of NavPress Publishing Group.

Scripture quotations marked (NIV) are taken from the *Holy Bible, New International Version®*, NIV®. Copyright © 1973, 1978, 1984 by Biblica, Inc.™ Used by permission of Zondervan. All rights reserved worldwide. www.zondervan.com

Scripture quotations marked (NKJV) are taken from the *New King James Version*. Copyright © 1982 by Thomas Nelson, Inc. Used by permission. All rights reserved.

Scripture quotations marked (NLT) are taken from the *Holy Bible, New Living Translation*, copyright © 1996. Used by permission of Tyndale House Publishers, Inc., Wheaton, Illinois 60189. All rights reserved.

This novel is a work of fiction. Names, descriptions, entities, and incidents included in the story are products of the author's imagination. Any resemblance to actual persons, events, and entities is entirely coincidental.

The opinions expressed by the author are not necessarily those of Tate Publishing, LLC.

Published by Tate Publishing & Enterprises, LLC
127 E. Trade Center Terrace | Mustang, Oklahoma 73064 USA
1.888.361.9473 | www.tatepublishing.com

Tate Publishing is committed to excellence in the publishing industry. The company reflects the philosophy established by the founders, based on Psalm 68:11,
"The Lord gave the word and great was the company of those who published it."

Book design copyright © 2014 by Tate Publishing, LLC. All rights reserved.
Cover design by Gian Philipp Rufin
Interior design by Gram Telen

Published in the United States of America

ISBN: 978-1-63418-084-9
1. Fiction / Christian / General
2. Religion / Christian Life / Personal Growth
14.10.08

To my darling Mia.

Contents

Preface

My teenage years were pretty rough. My body started changing, hormones were active, and I was on the brink of having feelings for boys; weird feelings. They started looking cute even though I really didn't like them. They got on my nerves, and they smelled like they never bathed. I hated what was going on with my body. The menstrual cycle commencement was a nightmare. I never knew I had so much blood. My breast and hips started to explore the outer regions of my body. My favorite straight-legged Levi's jeans no longer fit. I was frustrated. My mom told me about some things, don't get me wrong, but I had to go through this season of my life for a reason; all of us girls do. It's part of maturity.

We go through a lot in our teenage years. If there is something missing in our lives, then we look to others to get it. I ask that you look to Jesus. Before you slam doors in your parents' face because you feel they don't understand you, read this book. Before you decide to run away from home because you just don't get your way and your parents are splitting up, read this book. Before you fornicate with your boyfriend or take that first puff of street drugs, read this book. Before you consider cutting yourself because you hate who you are and because someone called you *stupid* and *worthless*, read this book.

Can I tell you that there is an enemy against you, his name is *Satan*. He wants to you steal, kill, and destroy your life because he enjoys it. He will entice you with what makes you feel good—drugs, alcohol, sex, and cutting yourself. He wants to remove you from God's truth because if you find out what God has for you then Satan can't touch you. Well, I am here to tell you that Satan can't have you. Satan has been trying to abort the plan that God has for his children for thousands of years. he tried with Moses, he has tried with the Jewish nation in the book of Esther, and he tried with Jesus. Can I tell you something else? Satan was defeated at the cross.

> The thief comes only in order to steal and kill and destroy. I came that they may have and enjoy life, and have it in abundance (to the full, till it overflows).
>
> John 10:10 (AMP)

There is a God who made you. The Lord knows you and cares about you. He knows the details of every second of your life. He wants you. He wants a relationship with you. He wants to bless you until you can't take it anymore. You are worthy to be loved and he is your man. I challenge you to stop breathing and try Jesus. He owns everything, is everywhere, and knows everything; once you check him out, you can't refuse.

> But He Who is coming after me is mightier than I,
> Whose sandals I am not worthy or fit to take off or
> carry; He will baptize you with the Holy Spirit and
> with fire.

Matthew 3:11 (AMP)

I pray that this book helps you understand that you are wonderfully and beautifully made by the hand of God. God loved us so much that he gave his only son for your salvation, an eternal relationship with him. The Lord wants you to know that he is not angry with you. He wants you to know that he loves you dearly, and you are important to him. He is attentive to the details in all areas of your life, your physical, emotional, mental, and spiritual well-being. The Lord is your father. He is a loving father.

I grew up without a father in the home. My parents divorced a year after I was born. He acknowledged my sisters as his own, but not me. I used to feel like I was some mistake. I wasn't daddy's little girl. I didn't know what that meant until I met my college roommate, moving into our dorm room freshman year. When I gave my life to Christ, which was well into my twenties, He revealed to me his fathering characteristics. I felt loved, cherished, forgiveness, special, beautiful, and most importantly I felt like someone's daughter. I hope that you see who he is and who he can be in your life. I believe he can change your life and eventually you can change your world and the world around you.

I Belong to Him

I love the fall. It's great. I know summer is over and we are back to school, but it's something about the cool weather and pulling out my sweaters, corduroy skirts and my funky tights. I love the sound of the dried leaves beneath my feet. What beautiful colors are made in the fall. When the seasons change, it seems like with them there is always something new.

My name is Nicolette. I'm in eighth grade, and I'm on my way to meet my mentor, Ms. Ruthie. I meet her at our church every Tuesday after school. Our church has an after-school program. Sometimes I feel I'm too old to attend this program, but I like hanging out there and a few of my friends attend also. Other kids play basketball, dodge ball, and practice their dance ministry routines. Some kids finish up their homework in the community room. There are several mentors in the after-school program. I choose Ms. Ruthie because I like the way she worships in service and always has a smile on her face. She loves the Lord. You can tell. I want whatever she has.

I meet with Ms. Ruthie because she is a cool, old lady, and she gives me good advice. Since my mom and I have a rocky relationship, she thought it would be good if I meet with Ms. Ruthie. My mom doesn't think I listen to her. Perhaps she means well, but she is too cuddly. I'm growing up. She says I'm growing up too fast. My mom is always cautioning me about my friend choices, clothes, and my behavior as I am becoming a young lady.

Ms. Ruthie and I have a great friendship. She teaches me some things that happened in her life when she was younger. A lot of things were different in her day. But you know boys are, always the same no matter what generation. They are smelly, silly, and immature. I don't understand why we girls like them and want their attention.

Ms. Ruthie is what the church folks call a *seasoned saint*. She is a senior citizen giving back to the community with her wisdom. She wears cool sneakers. She walks daily and talks to God. She calls them *prayer walks*. Sometimes another sister in the Lord goes with her. She is a mother, a grandmother, and she is still married, too.

"Hi, Ms. Ruthie!"

"How are you, Nicolette? How was school today?"

"It was okay. I got Algebra homework and Spanish vocabulary words to study."

"I'll be right with you to start our session. I'm finishing up our mentoring paperwork."

"Okay let's get started."

Ms. Ruthie's eyes twinkle when she smiles. I think her dentures are so white. She must use that denture cream stuff on a regular basis. You can tell she loves the Lord. Some other ladies in the church said she is carrying the *fire*.

We are talking about being a part of God's family today. I sometimes get sleepy when she shares a scripture with me. I sometimes don't understand it. She explains it to me though. She is teaching me to ask the Holy Spirit to help me, when I read the Bible on my own.

"So let's see where did we end last week?"

"I believe we're talking about the family of Jesus."

"Do you know, Nicolette, that the word of God has everything you need for living this life?" It's a living document of wisdom for every need. It's the Lord speaking to us."

"Yes, Ms. Ruthie, you already told me, several times."

"Now, Apostle Peter was sharing the Gospel with Cornelius and his family in Acts 10. Peter had learned that the Lord is no respecter of persons. All persons are received and accepted into the kingdom of God. Peter also learned that it's not of God to call anyone common or ordinary. While Peter was preaching about Jesus, the Holy Spirit came upon Cornelius and his family. The Jews that traveled with Peter were amazed that the Holy Spirit hit the gentile family. Peter charged them to be baptized in the name of Jesus."

"So, Nicolette, who are the gentiles?"

"We are the gentiles, non-Jews."

"That's right. Not only were the Jews able to hear, and receive the Gospel but we are, too. The Lord made it clear to Peter and the Jews in Acts 10:34–35. Therefore the Gospel of Jesus Christ is preached all over the world to ever man, woman, and child no matter what race, religion, rich, or poor."

"So what does it mean now that I'm saved; that I'm in the Lord's family?"

"It means that you have the same promises, privileges, and anointing that the Jews who followed Jesus were given. Let's look at Acts 11:17."

> "As I began to speak," Peter continued, "the Holy Spirit fell on them, just as he fell on us at the beginning. Then I thought of the Lord's words when he said, 'John baptized with water, but you will be baptized with the Holy Spirit.' And since God gave these Gentiles the same gift he gave us when we believed in the Lord Jesus Christ, who was I to stand in God's way?"
>
> Acts 11:15–17 (NLT)

"Peter learned that the Lord has made his Gospel available to the gentiles. The Lord has called us into his family with the same privileges as the Jews. And Romans 8:15–16 says,"

> So you have not received a spirit that makes you fearful slaves. Instead, you received God's Spirit when he adopted you as his own children. Now we call him,

"Abba, Father." For his Spirit joins with our spirit to affirm that we are God's children.

Romans 8:15–16 (NLT)

"Do you see, Nicolette? You're a member of God's family. You can call him Father. Do not let anyone tell you that you're not. The word of God says upon your salvation through Jesus Christ, you're now grafted into his family. You're a coheir to the throne. The Holy Spirit, the Spirit of God, teaches us that we belong to the Lord through Christ Jesus. So it's the Lord that has the plans for your life, your destiny. No one knows the plans for your life best but God himself. Some people may speak into your life and try to manipulate your decisions, but the most important thing you must remember is—God has the final say. Anything you see or hear that doesn't agree with God and his Word must be rejected. Everything must line up with the word of God. This is a great time for you to develop your relationship with him, and train your ear to his voice."

"So I belong to him and he belongs to me, right?"

"Yes that's right, Nicolette. You're a child of the King of Glory! He loves you very much!" Ms. Ruthie smiled. I thought she was going to get up and do one of her worship dances.

"Okay, Ms. Ruthie, I get it. This is kinda cool. I have a great big father in the sky."

"No, he's not in the sky, Nicolette, he's with you always. His spirit lives inside of you. He's not in some faraway land.

He's with you every moment of your life. He knows and sees what you go through, even your thoughts. Turn with me to Psalm 139:1–5, let's read:"

> O LORD, you have examined my heart and know everything about me. You know when I sit down or stand up. You know my thoughts even when I'm far away. You see me when I travel and when I rest at home. You know everything I do. You know what I am going to say even before I say it, LORD. You go before me and follow me. You place your hand of blessing on my head. And we have received God's Spirit (not the world's spirit), so we can know the wonderful things God has freely given us.
>
> Psalm 139:1–5 (NLT)

"And Galatians 5:25 says we're to live by his Spirit. His spirit guides us in everything."

> Since we are living by the Spirit, let us follow the Spirit's leading in every part of our lives.
>
> Galatians 5:25 (NLT)

"All you have to do, Nicolette, is to seek him in everything, believe, and live a holy life, as he is holy."

> Seek the Kingdom of God above all else, and live righteously, and he will give you everything you need.
>
> Matthew 6:33 (NLT)

"I'm giving you some homework this time, Nicolette. I want you to meditate on these three scriptures and write down how it makes you feel. What are some things that you can do to grow your relationship with God?"

"Okay, I'll get on them. These scriptures make me feel special to God. I've never seen them before."

"Well, that's good, it pleases God when you put your faith in him and know that he's with you, not against you."

"Tell me how school's going for you?"

"It's okay. I feel like I don't fit in. I feel like I'm an outsider. Why's that, Ms. Ruthie?"

"Well you're different because you belong to Christ. You're chosen and selected by him. Not everyone's the same, Nicolette, even those chosen by God. You must ask the Lord to help you see you through his eyes."

"Huh?"

"Ask the Lord to open your eyes to how he sees you. I found in my life that who I am was not how God saw me. I felt rejected, isolated, ugly, fat, and lacked confidence in my work. But I wanted to know who I was in God's eyes; what God thought of me. When he shared with me through his Word who I was and what I looked like to him, my thoughts about myself changed. He said, "I could do all things through Christ Jesus." My attitude pertaining myself and my capabilities changed. I didn't rely or depend on what others said or thought about me, even my closest friends. What the Lord said meant much more to me because I knew I belonged to him. I felt his love for me and that was all that mattered.

"In my walk with the Lord, Nicolette, well it hasn't been a bed of roses. I've lost some things along the way. I even lost friends and family members. It brought me tears and heartache to lose them, but I wanted to stay my course with the Lord. Every time I lost something or someone special to me, the Lord was always there to comfort me. He showed up, wiped my tears, and picked me up. He brought me new relationships, new jobs, and most importantly more revelation of who he is. I got to know him better and better as I went through those tough circumstances."

"Hey, Ms. Ruthie, in being a part of God's family, are you saying that there'll be some family drama like at my family reunion? Uncle Charlie and Cousin Theo always fight after playing cards. They seem to fight over the same thing every year. I think they're going to be mad at each other for the rest of their lives."

"Yes, I'd say there's some family drama, hopefully not to the extreme of Uncle Charlie and Cousin Theo, but there may be some tension from time to time. But that doesn't mean that it can't be resolved in a godly manner. Just remember, Nicolette, that the Holy Spirit, God himself is within you to help you. He'll guide you, not abandon you. So if you need help or answers, just seek him and ask. He listens and is attentive to reply."

Your Turn

Review the Scriptures that Ms. Ruthie gave Nicolette. The Scriptures are Psalm 139:1–5, Galatians 5:25, and Matthew 6:33.

1. What do they mean to you?

2. How do they make you feel?

3. Are you being led by the Holy Spirit? What changes can you do in your life to allow the Holy Spirit to lead you?

My Beauty on the Outside

I went home and worked on the Scriptures that Ms. Ruthie gave me. I think it's kinda cool that God is interested in me. He knows my feelings, thoughts, plans for the future, everything. That night, I thought about what Ms. Ruthie said about how she used to feel about her body and her confidence. It's amazing that I have those thoughts, too. I wish my friends would see me as I am and not by what I wear or look like. I know my mom is doing the best she can to buy clothes for me. Sometimes we have to just buy the ordinary jeans, not the sparkle skinny jeans, like my friends have. They put cool shirts on with their skinny jeans. I don't know why all the cool, fancy clothes are so expensive. When they go on sale, which is after the season is over, then my schoolmates say "you're out of style." It's hard to keep up.

Some of those clothes I don't look right in. I have big boobs and my hips are rounded. I look like a pear in those skinny jeans anyway. This puberty thing sucks. During my cycle, I get cramps all the time and I feel ten pounds heavier. I hate going to PE class during my period. Changing in the locker room is so embarrassing. I always think that I had an accident. I prefer to change my clothes in the bathroom stall.

I don't like my body. I feel unattractive. Don't get me wrong, there are a few boys that look at me and ask my phone number, but they aren't the cute ones. All the cute boys are with the cheerleaders. I get smiles from the nerdy boys or those that are really shy. My mom wants me to befriend the Christian kids. I have a few at church. We hang out sometimes during dance ministry practice and after our performances.

I look at the girls at my school and they all have the latest fashion and the hair looks like it was done by a hairstylist. Some of them even paint their nails with black, green, or orange nail polish. I prefer the classic French manicure with topcoat polish. Some others girls that formed a clique wear more provocative clothing. These girls aren't at my school. I see them mostly at the mall or the stores my mom and I shop. My school doesn't allow low-cut shirts, shorts above the thigh, miniskirts, flip-flops, or tank tops. I watched them. These girls get the attention of the boys; actually boys much older than them.

I have a friend named Felicia. Her sister, Ashley, is two years older than she. Felicia used to dress showing her chest in low-cut shirts and her butt and hips in tight high-cut shorts. Some boys took a fancy to her and they ganged up on her and raped her at a party. She became pregnant at the age of fifteen. She doesn't dress like that anymore. She wanted to abort the baby, but decided to keep him. I felt bad for her. But in a way, I think she helped the situation by dressing like that. I've learned that boys don't respect you when you are provocative and in pursuit of them. They can pretty much have their way with you, and then dump you. Ashley is not what she used to be. She dealt with a violation of her body and newborn baby months after. She lost some of her friends and her parents are expecting her to raise the child, work, and go to college just as they did. I don't want to end up like Ashley it seems too much to handle.

I was getting my books out of the locker and thought to myself how is the Holy Spirit going to help me with the way I feel about myself? I headed outside to meet the bus. It was Tuesday again and I was anxious to meet with Ms. Ruthie.

"Hello, Nicolette, how was your week?"

"It was okay, Ms. Ruthie. I studied my Scriptures you gave me last week."

"Good job. Do you have any questions?"

"Yes, I do. How can the Holy Spirit help me feel good about myself; to know that I'm not strange or weird by what I wear or don't wear? I have a few friends, but we're not in the *cool* crowd. We're excluded because we aren't popular like them."

"Well, said Ms. Ruthie. I think what you're dealing with, Nicolette, is that you're comparing yourself to your peers. When you compare yourself to others, you tend to feel inferior, insecure, and discontent with yourself. These feelings that you have aren't what God wants you to struggle with. The Lord created everyone. We all have different fingerprints. Imagine all the people of the world having different fingerprints! Only God can do that! There's no need to compare yourself with others because God has given each and every person a gift, talent, an anointing for his purpose. He loves everyone individually."

"How many gifts, talents, and anointing does God have?"

"Plenty for all. God made you special with your own uniqueness, beauty, personality, gifts, and talent. The Lord wants you to feel good about yourself because he made you. Remember last week I wanted you to ask the Lord to help you see what he sees in you. Did you ask the Lord, Nicolette?"

"I haven't, Ms. Ruthie."

"Okay, would you like it if I prayed with you and ask him together? Are you comfortable with that?"

"That would be great, Ms. Ruthie! Yes, let's ask him together!"

"Okay, let's close our eyes and pray together."

> Heavenly Father, I pray that you show Nicolette how you see her. Show her, Lord, that she's beautifully made by your wonderful hand. Open her eyes to see what you see in her. We petition you, Lord, that you continue to reveal your Word in her life and the Holy Spirit will teach and guide her according to your will and plan. Forgive us, Lord, for comparing ourselves

to others and give us the hearts of gratitude for the blessings you bestowed upon us; in Jesus' name. Amen.

"Amen!" I said. "I feel pretty good, Ms. Ruthie. I know that God's going to help me. I learned last week that I'm part of his family. So if I'm part of his family then he cares enough for me to help me. But, sometimes I feel down because I don't have the looks or things my classmates have."

"Don't worry, Nicolette. It's our human nature to sometimes feel down about ourselves, but the key is to get up on the inside. Through prayer and reading the Word, the Holy Spirit is working on you already."

"Get up on the inside?"

"Yes, it's important that whenever you're feeling down, you get up on the inside, meaning you have to think on positive things. Turn your thoughts around for the good. I recently read online that 75 percent of girls with low self-esteem engage in negative and harmful activities such as eating disorders, cutting themselves, bullying, smoking, drinking, and premarital sex.[1]

"You see, Nicolette, when you're feeling down about yourself, these are not remedies that God intended for you to take part in. These activities are harmful to your body and others and really don't make you feel better. Beware of these activities, Nicolette, they're life destroying and have deadly consequences. King David gives an example of getting up on the inside."

Why are you cast down, O my inner self? And why should you moan over me and be disquieted within me? Hope in God and wait expectantly for Him, for I shall yet praise Him, Who is the help of my [sad] countenance, and my God.

Psalms 43:5 (AMP)

"King David was facing some injuries by his enemies, not only was he hurting on the outside, he's also hurting on the inside. He's questioning himself as to why he was down and depressed. David shares with us here that he places his hope in God. For he knows the Lord is his help. You may have learned this in Sunday school that King David was a man after God's own heart. He was very close to the Lord and cherished their relationship. As we have seen in the Scriptures, the Lord was faithful in his friendship with David even when he wasn't. So David was able to draw on the Lord despite his sin, God remained in relationship with David through the good times and the bad."

"So are you saying that when I feel bad about myself, that I must talk to God, tell him how I feel and he'll help me feel better?"

"Yes, Nicolette, talk to God, let him know what you're feeling. He already knows what you've been facing, but he loves for you to come to him and talk. That's what prayer is all about, talking and listening. It's conversing with the almighty God about anything and everything you are going through in your life. You talk to your friends on the phone, don't you?"

"Yes, I talk a lot on the phone."

"Well, God wants to talk to you the same way. The best part about talking to the Lord is that his lines are free and always open 24/7. You'll always get love, not judgment or condemnation. He'll love you always no matter the sin done by you or to you."

"Wow. Jesus will always be there for me, huh?"

"Yes, nothing can separate the love he has for you (Romans 8:38–39). Another way that God speaks to you is through his Word, the Bible."

"Yes, I remember Pastor Mitchell always tell us to read and study the Word."

"That's right. The word of God has everything you need for everything in your life. It's a living word. It has promises specifically for you, Nicolette. These promises are good, not to harm you. So there's really no reason to bring harm to yourself or others when the word of God is in your heart and is the foundation of your faith. Sometimes, Nicolette, when I feel down, I like to draw upon a Scripture from the Bible to anchor me."

"Anchor you?"

"Yes, I think of it like a boat with an anchor. The anchor is dropped far down to the sea floor to keep from tossing about on the waters. The word of God is like an anchor, it keeps us grounded and stable in the midst of storms or troubles in our lives. I want you to read Hebrews 6:17–20 when you get home.

> God also bound himself with an oath, so that those who received the promise could be perfectly sure that he would never change his mind. So God has given both his promise and his oath. These two things are unchangeable because it is impossible for God to lie. Therefore, we who have fled to him for refuge can have great confidence as we hold to the hope that lies before us. This hope is a strong and trustworthy anchor for our souls. It leads us through the curtain into God's inner sanctuary. Jesus has already gone in there for us. He has become our eternal High Priest in the order of Melchizedek.
>
> Hebrews 6:17–20 (NLT)

"Our session time together is running out, so I like to share with you what God says about comparing ourselves to others. Is it okay that I share this with you?

"Yes, Ms. Ruthie. I wanna know."

"Okay, let's look at Galatians 6:4–5."

> Each one should test their own actions. Then they can take pride in themselves alone, without comparing themselves to someone else, for each one should carry their own load.
>
> Galatians 6:4–5 (NIV)

"This scripture is saying you shouldn't value yourselves based on someone else's views or opinions. You shouldn't think lower or higher of yourself based on financials status, spiritual position, or knowledge base. It says to look to you, your actions and behavior that you remain in uprightness with God. One day all will have to give account for their actions to God.

"For example, in my day, we used to call comparing ourselves with others as "keeping up with the Joneses." What that means is many people look to what others had, for example their home. They in turn want what the Joneses have—a big house with all the fancy details and big yard with a swimming pool.

"Unfortunately, when they bought their house, a house as big as the Joneses, they got into tremendous debt. They had difficulty refinancing because they got into even more debt furnishing the home. The home was later foreclosed and the college fund account was emptied out for a new residence. So keeping up with the Joneses proved unwise because they couldn't enjoy what they had and came under a mountain of debt and even the children suffered."

"Do you understand this, Nicolette?"

"Yes, I think so, Ms. Ruthie. It sounds like if we live by someone else's dream, it doesn't mean that dream is for us. But if we ask God about our dream, he can make it come true."

"I think that's a good analogy. Don't misunderstand me. God wants you have the best things in life and you can have them, but getting those things his way will bring peace not trouble."

> We do not dare to classify or compare ourselves with some who commend themselves. When they measure themselves by themselves and compare themselves with themselves, they are not wise.
>
> 2 Corinthians 10:12 (NIV)

"Huh," I said.

"We shouldn't take pride in or boast of the things we have or who we are and be haughty toward others because of it. We should be thankful in what God has blessed us with. Apostle Paul kept to what God had blessed him with, which was to preach the Gospel wherever he went; helping others to know Jesus. He didn't boast in the gifts and anointing that God gave him. He remained thankful and humble before God even when he faced people who looked down upon him. He didn't dare move outside of what God gave him to appease others or give glory to himself."

"Oh, okay, I get it. Paul wasn't snotty and stuck-up because he was all that and a bag of chips! And he didn't want to be like the other folks because he knew that wasn't the right thing to do. He knew he was different because he preached Jesus and he was okay with it."

"That's right. Paul did not tangle himself up with other folks and attaining what they had. He was about God's business. When you're about God's business, none of that stuff matters. God supplies all your needs and gives you the desires of your heart. It's wise to seek God's counsel."

"Okay, one more scripture," she said. "Let's look at Romans 12:2."

> Do not conform to the pattern of this world, but be transformed by the renewing of your mind. Then you will be able to test and approve what God's will is— his good, pleasing and perfect will.
>
> Romans 12:2 (NIV)

"Here, Apostle Paul is saying don't conform to the patterns of this world. These patterns may be financial gain, educational prestige, lust of the flesh, power and control, changing how you look to please others, changing how you behave to fit in, the list goes on and on.

"He says to be renewed in your mind with the word of God. Remember the word of God has everything you need in life. When you allow and guide the word of God in your heart, you'll know God's will; his plan for you in every area of your life.

"I've learned that taking matters into my own hands proved more trouble for me and a delay in God's promise. There was a situation in my life where I felt God was taking too long in answering my prayer. So I took the matter in my own hands and resolved the issue. Unfortunately for me, it proved more trouble and I felt I missed God. I asked the Lord's forgiveness, he cleaned up the situation, and I learned to wait on God and to trust his plan for my life."

"We covered a lot today, Nicolette."

"No, it was good. I'm going to think about what you shared. I know that I shouldn't compare myself with others. Sometimes I ask God why I can't have those things."

"He wants you to trust him. You can have those things, Nicolette, and so much more. Just do it his way; you can never be disappointed. The Holy Spirit will help you understand these Scriptures, help you to remember them when you need them, and will help you see yourself as God sees you. You are so special to him and he loves you very much!"

"I'll remember. Nothing can take his love of me away."

"That's right. Have a good week and I'll see you next time. Bring back more questions, so we can discuss more."

Your Turn

Mrs. Ruthie gave Nicolette some great advice.

1. Have you compared yourself to others? How did it make you feel?

2. What Scriptures help you with comparing yourself to others?

3. How are you going to respond to peer pressure regarding your figure, choice of clothing, or hobbies? Recall some Scriptures previously discussed that can keep you encouraged on who you are to Jesus.

My Beauty on the Outside (Remix)

The next couple of days, for some reason, were tough for me. I was sitting in the cafeteria having my lunch with one of my best friend, Theresa. Lisa, one of the prettiest girls in school, came over to our table and poked fun at my outfit.

"Hey, nerdy girl, what're you wearing? Did your mama let you go out the house like that?" said Lisa.

"Excuse me?" I said.

"You heard me! You're nothing, you can't dress, and you can't dance," exclaimed Lisa.

Apparently Lisa knew I was on the dance team at church. I was kinda dressed up that day. I had on a pair of my jeans, a nice white blouse my mom bought me, and my ballet-like slippers with bows on them. Theresa and I were minding our business and here comes Lisa and her crew to bully me with her words. Theresa did not say a word and just shrieked into her lunch tray. I, on the other hand, gave Lisa my attention as she had offended me. This was not the first time she blew her horn about anything I do or wear.

"Well, Lisa," I said. "It's really none of your business what I have on, and if you're so interested in my clothes, why won't buy them for me."

Well I think I hit a nerve with Lisa. It was spaghetti day for lunch. I got Lisa's spaghetti on my new shirt. She poured it right on my shirt. She spoke a few obscene words and walked away. Theresa was shocked as I was and helped me clean my shirt off. Everyone in the cafeteria had their eyes on me. Some were laughing and sneering. Others felt sorry for me and ran over to get more napkins to clean my shirt. It was just one of those days. My mother is going to freak out when she sees my shirt.

I went the rest of the day, four more class periods with a tomato sauce stain on my shirt. It was so embarrassing. Some kids in the hallways were gossiping and laughing at my big, fat spot on my shirt. One of the boys I kinda have a crush on Brian, said that I missed my mouth. He smiled and walked away. I just stood there like a statue, wondering why he said that. He is so nice to me, but would not be caught eating or hanging out with me. I was hurt by his comment more than Lisa's rebuttal.

That afternoon felt like eternity. I finally went home. This wasn't my day to meet Ms. Ruthie. I just went home to contend with my mom.

I told my mom what happened since she saw my shirt in the laundry basket blaring red and white. She wanted to call Lisa's parents and tell them a thing or two. I told her not to make a big deal out of it. She said I handled myself well and that she was proud of me. My feelings were still hurt. I think I was mad and hurt at the same time. I was mad at Lisa and hurt by Brian. I had trouble focusing on my homework, but pushed myself through it. Theresa texted me to see how I was doing. I told her I was fine and that I didn't feel like talking. I went to bed with tears. I did not feel like praying to the Lord. I knew I should have but the events of the day were so overwhelming. I completely forgot all that Ms. Ruthie taught me in the last couple of weeks.

Well Tuesday came around again. I was anxious to tell Ms. Ruthie what happened last week with the spaghetti on my shirt. Lisa didn't mess with me anymore that week and the word in the hallways quickly change when someone else gets picked on or got expelled.

"Hello, Nicolette, how are you doing today?"

"Hi, Ms. Ruthie, we have to talk."

"Oh my, what's going on?"

"I got picked on again at school."

"Really, what happened?"

"Lisa, one of the pretty girls at school, came over to my lunch table and made fun of my outfit then threw spaghetti on my new white shirt."

"How did you respond?"

"Well she asked if my mom really let me out of the house looking like that. I replied that it was none of her business and that if she was so concerned with my clothes, she can buy them for me, then she threw the spaghetti on my shirt."

"Oh my, why do you think she picks on you?"

"I don't know," I replied. "I guess she's jealous or something. But I don't know why she would be jealous of me! Well that night I didn't feel like praying. I just went to bed in tears."

"Oh I see. I understand," said Ms. Ruthie. "There have been many times in my life where I didn't feel like talking to God, reading my Bible, or even worshipping him. I had such a bad day or bad week, sometimes I'd get into such a funk that it messes up my time with the Lord. I learned later after several occurrences that I didn't want anything or anyone to interrupt my relationship with God.

"It's okay, Nicolette. Don't beat yourself up over it. I think you responded well. Next time, however, try not to let her entice you in an argument or fight. You can ignore her or walk away or if you're at the lunch table eating just tell her she can speak to you at a later time; not while you're eating."

"But what if that doesn't work, Ms. Ruthie?" I asked.

"It'll work if you say a quick prayer. Say 'Jesus, move her from me,' or 'Jesus, please handle this situation now.' You can say it very quietly. I know Jesus will rescue you out that situation. You'd be amazed, Nicolette, how fast God moves on your behalf! Well, I'm glad you shared that with me, Nicolette. You're brave. I believe that I know why she picks on you so much."

"Why's that, Ms. Ruthie?"

"It's because you're special, you have an anointing on your life."

"What does that mean?"

"It means that when you're called of God or have a God assignment on your life, the enemy, the devil will try to get you out of it by using his tactics to discourage you by walking away from God and the destiny he has for you. You can't see this, Nicolette, but I see it on you. I couldn't understand why I was picked on when I was a child. I never understood why till I got saved."

"You too?"

"Yes, I too didn't have nice fancy clothes, I wore glasses, and I was very short for my age. I was easy to pick on. I played the violin and viola in orchestra and was kinda nerdy. I was a tomboy, and rough around the edges, but I was still picked on. I just didn't understand why these two girls, whom I never hung out with, jumped me in the gym locker room. It was so weird, as if they had planned it."

"Well, Nicolette, I didn't know Jesus the way you do at your age." She chuckled. "They hit me, taking turns, and I hit them back. One moved away from my blow and the other came hitting. I tag team them, till the gym teacher broke us up. The two girls got in trouble. I didn't even get sent to the principal's office. The teacher knew that I didn't start the fight and was protecting me. I kept to myself. She knew those girls were up to no good."

"Wow, Ms. Ruthie. I would've never thought you beat up people."

"My mom taught us girls to protect ourselves. If someone hit you, then hit them back. I still believe in it. But now that I'm with the Lord, I have to be careful how I pick my battles. Most of them are not for me to fight, but for God to avenge. I have to be ready and quick to say sorry and forgive them, so that Jesus can forgive me."

"Gee, Ms. Ruthie, that must have been intense."

"Yes it was, and I was so upset and surprised by it that I had a hard time doing my homework that evening. I didn't come home with any injuries, so there was nothing to alarm my mom about."

"Now, Nicolette, you have a great big God inside of you and these girls and boys can't pick on you any longer. They can't pick on you because your response is Godly. When you have a godly response, then that confuses the enemy and they won't know what to do."

"How do I do that?"

"Say for example, your reply to Lisa would've been, 'Well thank you, Lisa, by the way your outfit is very nice. Did you get on sale at Macy's?' You see, she would not expect that answer from you. You expected you to fight back either verbally of physically after she blasted you with her harsh words."

"Hatred stirs us strife and contentions. Love covers the offense. Love prevents strife and restores peace. Let's look at some Godly wisdom."

> Hatred stirs up contentions, but love covers all transgressions.
>
> Proverbs 10:12 (AMP)

> A soft answer turns away wrath, but grievous words stir up anger.
>
> Proverbs 15:1 (AMP)

> A hot-tempered man stirs up strife, but he who is slow to anger appeases contention.
>
> Proverbs 15:18 (AMP)

> A [self-confident] fool utters all his anger, but a wise man holds it back and stills it.
>
> Proverbs 29:11 (AMP)

"I get it, Ms. Ruthie. Lisa's a big fat fool! She's always pickin' at folks that are not like her. She's just a big bully. She wants to be in the spotlight all the time. Wait one day she'll have mud on her face. I bet she won't like it if she was laughed at."

"Nicolette, please don't call her a fool and don't wish her harm. But pray for her and forgive her offenses towards you. Remember what we talked about last week; keep focused on being in right standing with Jesus. It's for your best to forgive Lisa so Jesus can forgive you.

The Bible, the word of God says to forgive so you can be forgiven. Many people from generations to generation do not forgive others and have missed their calling, anointing, and maybe heaven because of unforgiveness in their hearts. Did you know that unforgiveness can lead to bitterness and even illness in your body?"

"Really?"

"Oh yes, it can, so make sure that you confess your sins to God. If you need help in seeing your sin, the Holy Spirit will definitely bring it into the light; or in other words reveal it to you. The Holy Spirit convicts us of our sins. He'll nudge us in our spirit and our consciousness when we're doing the wrong thing or about to get into a mess that we should not partake in."

"Do you see that a soft reply turns away wrath?"

"I do see that."

"So, you see it's not good to compare yourself to others. She may be dressed well on the outside, but she's not so pretty on the inside."

"Wow, I really see that. I've nothing to worry about. She's ugly on the inside. Those clothes, nails, and hair don't mean anything. I bet her friends would abandon her if they weren't afraid of her. There's one more thing I didn't share with you, Ms. Ruthie."

"What's that, Nicolette?"

"What Brian said to me."

"Who's Brian and what did he say?"

"Brian's this really cute guy at my school. I have English and social studies with him. I kinda have a crush on him. I was heading to my sixth-period class and he walked by me. He smiled and said I missed my mouth. I stopped and stood there frozen. I couldn't believe he said that to me. I was so embarrassed."

"I see. How did that make you feel?"

"I was hurt by it, Ms. Ruthie. I want him to like me. I looked like a clown with my shirt a total mess."

"Well, Nicolette, don't get too upset. If he understands, then he would know that accidents happen to people. Did he witness the incident?"

"I don't know. I'm sure he heard about it though."

"Well, this too shall pass. He'll forget about it. He'll also learn that you responded well in the situation. Is he pleasant with you or is he awry?"

"No, he is very pleasant with me. He says hello from time to time. We really don't speak much."

"Well, Nicolette, you'll have to forgive them both, as we spoke earlier. Release them to Jesus. Give Jesus your hurt and pain and he'll turn your tears to joy (Psalm 30:5). This is what Jesus says about forgiveness."

> For if you forgive people their trespasses [their reckless and willful sins, leaving them, letting them go, and

giving up resentment], your heavenly Father will also forgive you.

But if you do not forgive others their trespasses [their reckless and willful sins, leaving them, letting them go, and giving up resentment], neither will your Father forgive you your trespasses.

Matthew 6:14-15 (AMP)

"Wow, Ms. Ruthie, this was great. I feel a load off my shoulders for sharing this with you. I ask that Jesus help me with forgiveness."

"He'll help you, Nicolette. He already knows that you're willing to forgive. You'll know that you've forgiven them when you don't feel any resentment, animosity, or ill will towards them. You'll not want to take revenge upon them. You'll ask the Lord to bless them and you'll be at peace with them. Even though they may come against you again; you must again forgive them. In some cases, they may not apologize or ask for your forgiveness, but you must still forgive them, Nicolette."

So watch yourselves! "If another believer sins, rebuke that person; then if there is repentance, forgive. Even if that person wrongs you seven times a day and each time turns again and asks forgiveness, you must forgive."

Luke 17:3–4 (AMP)

"I understand, Ms. Ruthie. I'll work on the forgiveness because I don't want to miss what God has for me. Pastor Mitchell spoke about forgiveness last month. He said if we harbor unforgiveness, then we set ourselves up for missing God."

"Yes, that's absolutely right. You know all these things we've been talking about affects us on the inside. Did you notice that we dealt with feelings, emotions, anger, and meanness? Although your concern was with the outwardly appearance of your classmates, you've seen what really is going on the inside. We can talk more about that next time."

"Yep, I don't want to be like Lisa and her gang or even Brian. Yeah, they may look good in their hip clothes and have cool friends, but I don't want to be like 'em."

"Okay, Nicolette, I'll see you next time. Keep your head up! You're doing an outstanding job. Jesus is proud of you and how you're growing closer to him."

"Thanks Ms. Ruthie, love ya, bye!"

"Love you, too!"

Your Turn

Forgiveness is one kingdom principle that Jesus wants us to put in practice.

1. Think about those that may have hurt your feelings or did you wrong. Have you forgiven them?

2. Do you feel any anger, sadness, resentment, or ill-will toward them? If so, then you have to forgive them, so you can be forgiven.

3. Suppose you face that person who hurt you again? The true test of forgiveness is your response to them. Examine yourself to see if you are at peace when you come across them in future.

My Beauty Within

I went home from Ms. Ruthie's session feeling free; like a weight was lifted off my shoulders. Some of the things she said I didn't want to do, like forgive Lisa and Brian for humiliating me, but I knew deep down inside I had to do it so I can be completely free. I gritted my teeth and swallowed her instruction; actually God's instruction. She is so easy to talk to and I find myself not falling asleep when she speaks, unlike Pastor Mitchell. I hear some things that my Pastor says, but sometimes I get sleepy or find myself daydreaming or wandering away in thought. Ms. Ruthie nips things in the butt. Perhaps it's the way she shares her life or she is talking to me versus preaching to me. She sympathizes with me, but she gives me the truth no matter what. I wish I can take her to school with me so she can see firsthand how obnoxious things get sometimes.

I went back to school the following week feeling renewed. I think I realized that my body isn't so bad after all. It's what's inside that matters. I thought Lisa and Brian were the most beautiful people. They have everything; they live in nice homes, have the best clothes, and have many friends to hang with. But there is something that they are missing. There is something that made those things look smaller. I saw it when they spoke harshly to me. I realized I really didn't want what they had. It's a shame because Lisa and Brian both go to my church and they hear the same teaching I do.

I was thinking of going on a diet, but I like food too much. I need food. I burn it off in dance ministry anyway. Perhaps I could do a little bit more exercising. There is Zumba class here at the church on Thursday nights maybe I can join the class. That will work out great because my mom has choir rehearsal that night, too.

I'm on my way to meet Ms. Ruthie. We were stuck in traffic; looks like an accident is ahead of us. I hope my session won't be shortened because the bus is running late. I got to church twenty minutes late. Ms. Ruthie was waiting for me. The other kids went home or played while they waited for their parents to pick them up.

"Hello, Ms. Ruthie!"

"Hello ,Nicolette, how are you today? How was school?"

"It was good. There was no drama."

"Well that's good. I have this mentoring survey for you to fill out. Please answer the questions and return it to me in the envelope. I'll step out of the office while you do that."

"Ms. Ruthie, will we have our full session today? I'm sorry I'm late, there was an accident in front of the bus, and we got here late."

"Don't worry we'll have our full session today, Nicolette."

She stepped out of her office for a few minutes.

"Okay, Nicolette, have you completed your survey?"

"Yes, here you go."

"Okay, so where did we left off? How are you feeling about what we talked about last week?"

"We talked about my drama with Lisa and Brian. I had to forgive them. We talked about how I feel about my body briefly."

"So have you forgiven them, Nicolette?"

"I'm working on it. I know I haven't really forgiven them because I still didn't feel good when I saw them again at school. I still wanted them to get what's coming to them."

"Well, Nicolette, don't give up. Keep trying by praying and asking God for help. The Holy Spirit will help you, and then before you know it, you'll be completely over it, without ill feelings and you can be at peace with them."

"Those girls that jumped me in the girl's locker room; I had a difficult time forgiving them. I didn't know how to forgive. I remember hearing about it at church, but I did not know how to put it into practice, nor did I have a mentor to talk to. I really didn't have a relationship with God. I just went to church because my grandmother dragged me to church.

"I was on edge with those girls weeks following the incident. I thought they were going to try to get back at me because I got the last round of hits in and they got in trouble with the principal. So I too was tense and was ready to defend myself again if they wanted to retaliate."

"So what happen?"

"Well, as time passed it was forgotten. My classmates forgot; the girls went about their business and so did I. Nothing else happened between them and me. There was always drama at school. It was always someone else's turn to get picked on or in trouble.

"It wasn't until I got saved and gave my life to Jesus that I learned what Jesus said about forgiveness. Once I read the Scriptures and realized that when I got saved, all my sins were washed away by the blood of Jesus; by the cross. For me to be in right relationship with Jesus, I had to forgive all those that offended me. I wanted to make things right. I wanted to start my relationship off with a clean slate."

"Have you heard of the expression 'junk in the trunk,' Nicolette?"

"Yep, I heard Pastor Mitchell speak about it."

"Well, 'junk in the trunk,' is an expression where you're carrying a lot of baggage from your past. The Lord wants us to drop our baggage at the foot of the cross. He's forgotten it through Jesus Christ and so should we. So if we're carrying anything from our past, like hurt, pain, or unforgiveness, we must lay it at the foot of the cross and let go and forgive; no matter how bad the person hurt you, Nicolette, you have to let go and forgive, that's including forgiving yourself."

"Do you remember the story of the paralyzed man, where his friend made a hole in the roof and lowered him in front of Jesus?"

"Yes, I remember that story in Sunday school."

"Well Jesus forgave him of his sin and the man was also healed. The religious Pharisees accused Jesus of blasphemy because he forgave and healed the once-paralyzed man. Look what it says in Mark 2."

> Then they lowered the man on his mat, right down in front of Jesus. Seeing their faith, Jesus said to the paralyzed man, "My child, your sins are forgiven."
>
> But some of the teachers of religious law who were sitting there thought to themselves, "What is he saying? This is blasphemy! Only God can forgive sins!"
>
> Jesus knew immediately what they were thinking, so he asked them, "Why do you question this in your hearts? Is it easier to say to the paralyzed man 'Your sins are forgiven,' or 'Stand up, pick up your mat, and walk'? So I will prove to you that the Son of Man has the authority on earth to forgive sins." Then Jesus turned to the paralyzed man and said, "Stand up, pick up your mat, and go home!"
>
> Mark 2:5–11 (NLT)

"Jesus forgives right on the spot huh?" I said.

"Yes, it was through the man's faith that he received forgiveness and healing. He had faith in Jesus Christ. It's by faith that we receive from the Lord our salvation, forgiveness of sin, healing, deliverance, peace, and all that God has for us."

"Yep, Jesus was popular with the crowds and poor folks because he's helping them in their need. People were running to him with all their sickness and stuff. Oh wait, I get it now. They ran to Jesus with all their junk in their trunk and asked for Jesus to bless 'em right?"

"That's right. We can come to Jesus the same way."

"The Lord made a new covenant with his people when he found fault with them."

"Yes, I remember that Adam messed it up for us," I interrupted. "I heard that Jesus is the last Adam."

"Yes, Nicolette. By Jesus going to the cross and raising on the third day, we're in new covenant with God. In this new covenant, our sins are forgiven and forgotten and all the blessings from the Lord are ours. Look at book of Hebrews 8.

> And I will forgive their wickedness, and I will never again remember their sins."
>
> Hebrews 8:12 (NLT)

"I know, Nicolette, we have spoken a lot about forgiveness. It's so important that we do all that Jesus teaches us."

"I understand, Ms. Ruthie. You know what?"

"What?"

"I don't want to be like Lisa and Brian. They have nice clothes and big houses and get nice stuff for Christmas, but I don't wanna be like them. I know now that it's wrong to compare myself to them."

"What changed your mind, Nicolette?"

"Well it's their behavior, the way she acted."

"You mean their character?"

"Yes, I don't like the way they act, so the things they have don't appeal to me. Lisa was so mean. She looks ugly when she's mean."

"And what about after she's mean, is she still ugly?"

"No, but I see her differently. I see what she really is and the stuff on the outside of her don't seem all that anymore."

"I see," Ms. Ruthie replied. "Well don't judge her, but just know that she has some things she has to work on (Matthew 7:1, AMP). We all fall short of the glory of God (Romans 3:23, AMP). We all have some things within us that we have to improve. We're not perfect. God's perfecting us (Philippians 1:6, AMP).

"You see, I met a wonderful woman who's also a seasoned saint. She was not the most beautiful woman on the outside. She has wrinkles around her eyes; she was humped over from osteoporosis. Her teeth weren't the whitest and her hair was thinning. But you know what; it wasn't the outer appearance that one would say she was beautiful. It's what was on the inside of her. She spoke with the love of Christ. She was gentle in her spirit. I don't believe she gets mad at anyone. When someone offended her, she'd return their comment in love, not striking back in harshness. Do you know what I mean, Nicolette?"

"Wow."

"She was truly living by the spirit of God. She was not offended by what people thought or said to her. I think she understood the character of the fruits of the spirit. Let's look at them briefly.

> When you follow the desires of your sinful nature, the results are very clear: sexual immorality, impurity, lustful pleasures, idolatry, sorcery, hostility, quarreling, jealousy, outbursts of anger, selfish ambition, dissension, division, envy, drunkenness, wild parties, and other sins like these. Let me tell you again, as I have before, that anyone living that sort of life will not inherit the Kingdom of God.

> But the Holy Spirit produces this kind of fruit in our lives: love, joy, peace, patience, kindness, goodness, faithfulness, gentleness, and self-control. There is no law against these things!

> Those who belong to Christ Jesus have nailed the passions and desires of their sinful nature to his cross and crucified them there. Since we are living by the Spirit, let us follow the Spirit's leading in every part of our lives. Let us not become conceited, or provoke one another, or be jealous of one another.

> Galatians 5:19–26 (NLT)

"Here, Apostle Paul is talking about our sinful nature and fruits of the Holy Spirit. There are vast differences aren't they?" she asked.

"Yes. So if I do anything based on my sinful nature then I won't go to heaven?"

"If you continue in your sin and not repent, turning away from them then there are consequences of your sins and actions," she replied. "The Lord judges all, the good, and the bad in your life."

"Yikes, I better do right by God then."

"Yes, stay in right standing with God. It's simple; just be obedient to his Word. Look at the fruits of the Holy Spirit, love, gentleness, patience, and kindness. These are what that woman I met expressed. In her expression of the fruits of the Spirit, she was very pretty. She repented and crucified her old nature or sinful nature. I don't know who she was before she gave her life to Christ. It really doesn't matter. What really matters is that she's walking in the spirit of God.

"So, Nicolette, you're a beautiful girl! You don't need to dress yourself to satisfy others. Just be who God made you to be. Be yourself. Your beauty emanates from the inside out. Be happy with yourself."

> Oh yes, you shaped me first inside, then out; you formed me in my mother's womb.

I thank you, High God—you're breathtaking!
Body and soul, I am marvelously made! I worship in
adoration—what a creation!

You know me inside and out, you know every
bone in my body;

You know exactly how I was made, bit by bit, how
I was sculpted from nothing into something.

Like an open book, you watched me grow from
conception to birth; all the stages of my life were
spread out before you,

The days of my life all prepared before I'd even
lived one day.

Psalm 139:13–16 (MSG)

"King David praised God for how he was made. He's
special and so are you. Never let anyone tell you that you're
nothing. You're wonderfully made by God who's beautiful.
He knows you inside and out. To not feel good about
yourself is like telling God he messed up, he was wrong in
creating your features and who you are; this dishonors him."

And let the beauty and delightfulness and favor of
the Lord our God be upon us; confirm and establish
the work of our hands—yes, the work of our hands,
confirm and establish it.

Psalm 90:17 (AMP)

Honor and majesty are before Him; strength and
beauty are in His sanctuary.

Psalm 96:6 (AMP)

"The beauty of Jesus emanating from you is a testimony of the Lord. No matter what your body size, shape, color of skin, or handicap. Your beauty is from the Lord; he's beautiful."

"I understand, Ms. Ruthie. The Lord is not pleased when I say I hate my body or how I look, huh?"

"No, that's not pleasing to him. Remember to ask him to open your eyes to how he sees you, Nicolette. I know it will be glorious to you; something you'll never forget. No one can take away or change how God looks upon you, or how he feels about you."

"I see, Ms. Ruthie. You know I feel better. I think this is a Scripture that I may want to memorize." I exclaimed.

"Yes, you can put these Scriptures on sticky notes and put them on your mirror or refrigerator or wherever you need a quick reminder of his love for you."

"Since I was uniquely made by God, then there's really no reason for me to desire to be like someone else, huh? I mean I was blown away that everyone on the whole planet has different fingerprints. That's so cool; imagine that!"

"I believe we went over our time, I wanted you to understand forgiveness, and how beautiful you're on the inside and out. You're a very bright, Nicolette, and you understand the Scriptures; that's very good."

"Thank you so much, Ms. Ruthie. I'll see you next time."

"See you next time, Nicolette. Keep praying and believing!"

Your Turn

Do know how beautiful you are? Do you know how God sees you?

Pray this prayer with Nicolette:

> Lord you have wonderfully and skillfully made me. I thank you and praise you for my body type, my personality and all my features inside and out. Help me to see myself as you see me. I thank you for choosing me to be your child. I am beautiful because you are beautiful. I bless you and honor you. In Jesus name I pray. Amen.

My Body the Temple

I went home with a load off my shoulders, and I looked in the mirror in the bathroom. I looked at myself up and down and said, "I'm beautiful!" I think the sticky note idea was a great one. I ran into my room and before I forget what Ms. Ruthie had showed me in the Bible, I wrote down some Scriptures that would help me. I was sick and tired of being a second-class citizen around school. I didn't have to be either. It's all in how God sees me and how I see myself. What my friends or classmates think of me doesn't matter; except of course if they complement me. The bad stuff they say, well I can dismiss it because it's not in agreement with God says about me.

Next day at school, everyone was talking about a party at Cherise's house. Theresa and I didn't get an invitation. All the popular kids were invited. How do I know? Well news travels fast around Franklin Jr. High School. I was sitting in my last period of the day and David passes me a note in class. It said that I was invited to the Cherise's party this Saturday. Cherise is a cheerleader and is going steady with Billy who's on the football team. Billy is a sophomore at Roosevelt High School.

I didn't know what to expect from this note. I was surprised. I thought it was a joke. I turned and looked at David with a slight smile. David looked at me with a big grin and whispered, "I'm going." The day was finally over. As I was walking back to my locker, I ran into Theresa. I showed her the note. Her eyes got big.

"Are you going, Nicolette?"

"I don't know yet."

"Who gave you the note? Do you think it's for real?"

"I'm not sure."

Brian came up to us and interrupted.

"Oh good you got the note." said Brian.

"Was this note from you, Brian?" Theresa asked.

"Yep, by way of Cherise," he replied.

"Why was I invited?" I asked.

"Why not," answered Brian. "You're cool with it right? You're going aren't you, Nicolette?"

"I don't know yet," I said.

"Okay, well check you chicks later!" Brian said and left.

"Theresa, did you get an invitation?"

"No, I didn't get an invite. You know I don't fit into that crowd. They don't like girls with glasses and braces on their teeth."

"But, Theresa, you're beautiful, Ms. Ruthie taught about how we should look at ourselves as God sees us and…"

"That's okay, Nicolette, you go. I don't want to go. It doesn't feel right to me to go," said Theresa. "I'll see ya tomorrow."

"Okay, see ya."

After I got home I wasn't feeling well. My mom asked what was going on with me. I told her that I was invited to Cherise's party on Saturday. She frowned.

"When and where's this party?" she asked.

"Mom, it's at Cherise's house. It starts at 6:00 p.m."

"Is this a slumber party; just the girls?"

"No, Mom, it's a regular party with boys there, too."

"I don't want you going to this party, Nicolette. Are they planning on drinking?"

"I don't know mom."

"Who's the chaperone?"

"I don't know, but I can find out. Can I go, Mom?"

"I want to talk to her parents first and find out who's chaperoning this party."

"Okay."

The next day at school, I tried to ask around to see if the party will be chaperoned by a Cherise's parents. I kinda had to keep it cool because I didn't want them to think I was some childish kid that needed a chaperone, like sixth grade camp or something. Wouldn't you know I ran into Cherise in the cafeteria? I asked her if her parents were going to be present at the party.

"My dad is on a business trip. He won't be back till next Thursday," she said. "My mom will be there though."

"Can I get your number so I can RSVP properly?"

"Sure," she said.

She gave me her number and I was feeling a bit better about my mom letting me go.

"Will you be there, Nicolette?"

"Sure I think I can make it."

I went home and gave Cherise's number to my mom, so she can call her parents to check on her party. I waited patiently in my room, doing my homework, looking out the window, fixing my hair, looking in the closet for something to wear to the party, you know the usual waiting. My mom knocked and opened the door. She said she spoke to Cherise's parents. She sat on my bed and said I could go on one condition.

"You can go, Nicolette, on one condition; that you clean up your room and you have to be back by 9:30 p.m.," she said.

"Mom, 9:30?" I exclaimed. I thought, *How embarrassing is that?*

"Yes, 9:30, that's it."

"Okay."

"Is Theresa going with you?"

"No, Theresa doesn't want to go."

"Are you two still friends?"

"Yeah, Mom, Theresa just doesn't want to go."

"Okay," she said. "She smiled and walked out the room."

Well the next couple of days I got busy and cleaned up my room. I even did a few extra chores around the house. I clean and vacuumed my room, mopped the kitchen floor and finished the laundry. I was excited about the party, but kinda sad that Theresa wasn't going with me. She is my hangin' buddy.

I searched through my closet to find something to wear to the party. It was Saturday afternoon already and I still didn't know what to wear. I was getting a headache from my search for the perfect outfit. I remembered that Lisa and the girls at school made fun of my choice of clothing. I slumped on my bed, tired and feeling out of sorts about this whole party thing. I looked at the sticky note that was on my bedside table on my photo of me and the dance team. It said…

> You know me inside and out, you know every bone in my body; You know exactly how I was made, bit by bit, how I was sculpted from nothing into something.
>
> Psalm 139:15 (MSG)

I closed my eyes and thought how God must know what's going on with me right now. After all, he made me inside and out. I fell asleep. My mom came into my room.

"Nicolette, are you still going to the party?" she asked.

"Yikes, what time is it, Mom?"

"It's 5:15."

"Oh man! I must have fallen asleep."

"I'll meet you downstairs and I'll drive you over to Cherise's place."

I jumped up off my bed and threw on my shower cap, grabbed my towel, and ran inside the bathroom. I showered and ran back into my room. I combed through my closet again and narrowed my selection down to three possible outfits, then two, then the winner! I wore my skinny jeans and a shirt that fitted my figure my auntie gave to me, and my flat ballet slipper-style shoes. My shirt was kinda cool. It had sparkles and stuff on it. I think I looked hip enough. I put the curling iron to my hair and added lip gloss to my lips and off I went like a horse in Kentucky Derby start.

"You look pretty, dear," my mom said.

"Thanks, Mom," I said.

"Okay, now I'll be back to pick you up at 9:30, Nicolette."

"Mom, can you park a little down the street a bit when you come back to get me?"

"Sure I think I can do that." She smiled. "Have fun and remember to make the right choices."

My mom and I already had a talk about drugs, alcohol, and premarital sex; so that was a warning.

Cherise lived in a neighborhood with huge homes. She was in the fancy area of town. Her house was humongous. The party was around back on the deck and by the pool. There were a lot of kids there. Most of them were from my school. There were some older kids there, too. I found out that there were from Roosevelt High, friends of Cherise's boyfriend, Billy. Some of the girls looked at me and snickered. I paid them no mind and went over to Kevin and Sharon I knew from school.

"Hey, Nicolette, you just got here?" Kevin asked.

"Yep, how is it?" I asked.

"It's okay, not really digging the party, but it's good to get out of the house," Sharon said.

We were looking around checking out the scene. Some kids were dancin', others were jumping on Cherise's brother's trampoline, some were just sitting around talking and eating. Some other kids were pushing each other in the hammock like a swing. I went over and got something to eat. The man minding the grill wasn't Cherise's dad and I never saw her mom there. I later found out it was Cherise's uncle. He was pretty young to be an uncle. He looked like he was in his thirties, I guess. I got some barbeque and sat down with Brian, Sharon, Kim, and Kevin. We chowed down and had some laughs. Sharon, Kevin, and Kim are in the dance ministry with me. The punch had sherbet floating in it. It tasted pretty good, except it was pretty tart like the cold medicine my mom used to give me when I was a kid. I didn't like it.

The kids kept going back to the punch bowl. The party was getting pretty wild as the evening dragged on. We all did a few line dances. Some of the boys sat out and watched us. They all had these stupid grins on their faces. I felt like I was prime rib in a meat market and they had the barbeque sauce. Brian asked me to dance after the line dancin'. I was totally shocked. He looked a little dazed. I asked if he was alright. He said "yes" and started grabbing my hips and chest. I slapped him and walked away.

These kids were drunk. Sharon and Kevin were inside playing a video game in the sunroom. Kim was swingin' on the hammock with some high school dude. The music and the party itself got louder. Some kids started taking off their clothes while bouncing on the trampoline. I think it was time for me to go. I didn't want to compromise as my mom warned. It was nearing 9:30 anyway. So I ran inside to Sharon and Kevin and told them I was heading home. They decided to stay and finish their game. I ran over to Kim and asked if she had a ride home. She said no and began hugging on the high schooler. I pulled Kim off of him and the hammock and we ran outta there.

"Hey, Nicolette, what's going on?" Kim asked.

"It's time to go Kim. These kids are drunk. We're not supposed to be a part of drinkin' parties."

"Hey I saw you and Brian dancin'. I think he likes you," she said.

"I think he likes everybody in the state he's in." I replied. "Are you feelin' okay?"

"No not really. My head is spinning and my stomach aches."

"Oh boy, Kim, you're drunk. How much of that punch did you drink?"

"Are you sure? How do you know?"

"Because, Kim, it's on your breathe and how you're behaving."

"My daddy used to be an alcoholic."

"Okay, Kim, look at me. I need you to focus. My mom's going to give you a ride home and you have to play it cool while you're in the car, okay?"

She straightened her shoulders up and said "okay."

My mom came with perfect timing. The party was getting loud and I didn't want her to know about the drinking and whatever else going on in the party. Kim and I got in the backseat and my mom drove off.

"Mom, can we drop off Kim at her house?" I asked.

"Sure, just show me where she lives."

Kim kept it cool in the car. She was holding her legs and was squeamish. I think she had to go to the bathroom. We dropped her off. Kim ran into her house without saying good-bye.

"How was the party, Nicolette?"

"It was okay, Mom. I was ready to leave. It wasn't what I thought."

"Why was that? Did you see some of your friends there?"

"I saw some of them. The barbeque was good," I replied.

"You look so pretty tonight, Nicolette. Was there anything else you'd like to share with me?"

"No, Mom. I'm good."

I got home and got under my comforter. I didn't want to come out. I thought sure if my mom found out that drinking and carrying on was going on I would be in trouble for good. I was worried for Sharon and Kevin. I hoped they got outta there. I pray that Kim didn't get in trouble with her dad. He would be fuming if he found out that she was drinking. He knows what drinking does and by no means was he going to allow it with his kids. He testified at church last year that only Jesus rid him of alcoholism; he couldn't do it himself.

Well Tuesday came around and I was off to see Ms. Ruthie. I hope she would be proud of my right choices this weekend. I found out that Sharon and Kevin got home okay and that they got in trouble with their parents. When Sharon's dad got there, he actually walked in and saw the chaos. She pulled Sharon outta there and dropped Kevin off at home. Kevin's mom found out from Sharon's dad and he then got in trouble too. Kim's dad was the wiser. He knew when Kim walked in the door she was drunk. It was as if he had a nose for the stuff. It was like he was a bloodhound in the airport. Boy, Kim got in big trouble. Her dad is going to watch her like a hawk from now on. I bet she won't be going to anymore parties for decades.

"Hello, Nicolette, how was your weekend?" she asked.

"It was good, Ms. Ruthie. I went to a party."

"Oh yeah, how was it? Did you have fun?"

"Yes and no, the party had alcohol," I replied.

"Oh, I see. Did you partake of it?" she asked.

"No. I had some of the punch and it tasted like medicine so I didn't want anymore. I noticed that the kids were acting sillier than usual so thought it was best to get outta there. I didn't want to compromise on what mom and I discussed."

"What did you and your mom discuss?"

"Well several years back, I was eleven; my mom and I talked about sex, drugs, and alcohol. She said not to do any of it. I should wait till I get married for the sex and that drugs and alcohol would ruin my body and even my life."

"That was a very good talk, Nicolette," she replied. "What else happened at the party?"

"Well I grabbed Kim and we left. My mom picked us up at 9:30. I thought that the kids at school were going to tease me for leaving early, but I didn't hear a peep from them. Some of them got in trouble for drinking."

"Oh, I see."

"What's it about drinking and drugs that people think it's so cool, Ms. Ruthie?"

"Well it's a part of the world. Alcohol and drug use have been around for centuries. It's even in the Bible. The Bible says to not to take part in drunken behavior or do bodily harm to yourself. Drinking and drug use is really not cool. What profit does it have? Hundreds of people have died in drunk-driving accidents annually. People of all ages have been imprisoned, sick, or died from drug use and overdose. Children born to mothers using drugs or alcohol have been born under the influence; some survive through withdrawal, others don't make it."

"Goodness." I replied.

"There's a whole list of activities, Nicolette, that will keep you from your inheritance as children of God," she said. "Let's look at Paul's letter to the Corinthians."

> Don't you realize that those who do wrong will not inherit the Kingdom of God? Don't fool yourselves. Those who indulge in sexual sin, or who worship idols, or commit adultery, or are male prostitutes, or practice homosexuality, or are thieves, or greedy people, or drunkards, or are abusive, or cheat people—none of these will inherit the Kingdom of God. Some of you were once like that. But you were cleansed; you were made holy; you were made right with God by calling on the name of the Lord Jesus Christ and by the Spirit of our God.
>
> 1 Corinthians 6:9–11 (NLT)

> Run from sexual sin! No other sin so clearly affects the body as this one does. For sexual immorality is a sin against your own body. Don't you realize that your body is the temple of the Holy Spirit, who lives in you and was given to you by God? You do not belong to yourself, for God bought you with a high price. So you must honor God with your body.
>
> 1 Corinthians 6:18–20 (NLT)

> Don't you realize that all of you together are the temple
> of God and that the Spirit of God lives in you? God
> will destroy anyone who destroys this temple. For
> God's temple is holy, and you are that temple.
>
> 1 Corinthians 3:16–17 (NLT)

"Paul was warning the Corinthian church against sexual sins, debauchery (abusing alcohol), idolatry, and the like. The society of Corinth was practicing sins that are still going on today—drunken parties, prostitution, theft, and adultery to name a few. Sex is for marriage between and man and a woman (Genesis 2:22–24, NLT). The word of God says don't be deceived by living a life dwelling in these sins and think you're going to heaven."

"Wow. God means business. It's pretty self-explanatory."

"Yes he does, and yes it is. Repentance is required. Paul warns don't be a part of such activity and you're to repent. In other words, stop it, turn away from it, and run from it. Your body is the temple of the Holy Spirit. Drugs, alcohol, and premarital sex cannot reside in it also."

"You made a wise choice, Nicolette, to abstain from alcohol and other activities going on at that party."

> Those who love pleasure become poor; those who love
> wine and luxury will never be rich.
>
> Proverbs 21:17 (NLT)

"Those that love worldly pleasures and set their hearts on them in the end become poor and may even see death.

There's a choice for all to make; eternal life in Christ Jesus or eternal death.

"You're very important to the Lord, Nicolette. He loves you very much. He wants you to make the right choices. Choose Jesus. Choose his way to live your life and you'll be healthy, happy, prosperous, blessed in all that you do."

"I understand, Ms. Ruthie. It's hard when there's so much pressure from your friends to fit in and be a part."

"I remember when I was doing street ministry, and I stopped and ministered to a few young men walking down the street. Two of them had their pants down around their butt, exposing their underwear. Anyway, I stopped, smiled, and shared the Gospel with them. They were very respectful and listened intently. One of the three was captivated. The other two were not receptive. I asked the captivated one if he wanted to pray and receive Jesus in his life. You can easily tell that he was thinking about it and looking at his friends wondering what they would think about him praying.

His mind was in a tug-of-war between how he looked in front of his friends versus making Jesus Lord of his life. I said, "I know these are your friends, but you're the brave one. The Lord has a big plan for your life." Seconds later he gave his life over to Jesus. His friends walked away, slowly looking back, and sneering. He didn't care. I gave him a big hug and prayed a blessing prayer over him. He smiled and thanked me twice. I said it's not me; it's Jesus who now has your back for the rest of your life.

"So you see, when we make the decision to live for Jesus, we look different, act different, and may lose some friends in the process. But rest assured that the life you lead is temporary. It's where you want to spend eternity that needs to be addressed."

"Yes, Ms. Ruthie, I feel for him. I bet he's wondering if his friends were going to make fun of him and tell the whole school about it."

"I know the Holy Spirit will help him stay strong in the Lord."

"It feels good to feel loved and important to someone, Ms. Ruthie."

"It does feel good to be a part of a family and be loved. You're part of God's family and he'll love you always, no matter how much you mess up, sin, or get into trouble. His love for you never stops. It's important for many teens and young adults to know this about Jesus. So many misunderstand him and think that he's a big judge in heaven. But no, he's a loving father taking care of his creation, his children. Like any father, he wants the best for his kids. He's so close to you, Nicolette, that he's living inside of you. Your body houses his' Holy Spirit. So if you feel that you're alone and afraid, don't be. You have a great big God living inside of you."

"Ms. Ruthie, can you pray with me like you prayed with that boy on the street?"

"Nicolette, I thought you receive Christ already in church a few years back?"

"Yes I did, but I want to do it again,"

"Yes let's pray! Just repeat after me."

> Dear Lord, I know and believe that your son, Jesus Christ, died on the cross and rose on the third day for the forgiveness of my sins. Thank you, Lord, for forgiving me. Come into my heart and life and be my Lord and Savior. From this moment forward, I give you my life and dedicate myself to you. In Jesus' name I pray, Amen.

"Beautiful, Nicolette, I'm so proud of you!" she exclaimed.

"I know God has a wonderful plan for your life as you continue to be humble and reach for more of him. You belong to him. Let me pray a blessing over you."

Ms. Ruthie prayed a wonderful prayer over me that brought tears to my eyes. She claimed Luke 2:52 on me. The verse said that Jesus grew up with godly wisdom and favor with God and with others. If Jesus has it I can too. We then dismissed for the week. She gave me a hug and said "so long." She too had tears in her eyes and a big smile on her face.

Your Turn

1. Have you experienced the *party scene*?

2. Knowing what the Scriptures says about drunken behavior, drugs use, and sexual sins, what would you do differently?

3. Do you need Jesus? Just say the simple prayer that Nicolette did out loud and watch God move in your life. He loves you dearly and wants a relationship with you not just on Sundays, but everyday of your life.

> Dear Lord, I know and believe that your son, Jesus Christ, died on the cross and rose on the third day for the forgiveness of my sins. Thank you, Lord, for forgiving me. Come into my heart and life and be my Lord and Savior. From this moment forward, I give you my life and dedicate myself to you. In Jesus' name I pray, Amen.

Wisdom From On High

I went home from Ms. Ruthie's session so light and free. She doesn't judge me or condemn me because of my actions or thoughts. She just teaches and challenges me to be closer to the Lord. It's not hard to draw close to him. I learned that from her. For some reason, I thought it was this ceremonial or ritual thing, but it's not. It's just asking him into my life and my mess and willing to receive what he has to say and expects in the relationship. It's a father relationship. I don't have a father in my life, but I understand that I have the Lord as my father. He is more than enough. He is wealthy, healthy, and wise. He has a place for me in heaven. I just have to persevere to get it. Pastor Mitchell told us that God has a mansion with many rooms. He prepared a place for us already in heaven (John 14:1–4, NLT). That is comforting to know that one day I will see him and he is working on my crib. I just have to hold onto his hand through these years of my life.

I felt pretty bad about not going to the party with my best friend Theresa, having a drink at the party and witnessing what I had encounter. I felt that I really messed up with the Lord. But you know what, if I just tell him about and just be straight up honest with him, he listens and forgives me. I forgot that Ms. Ruthie said that he is everywhere and knows everything; so I guess that means the Lord knew I was going to the party and what I was getting myself into. Gosh, he still loves me no matter how much I screw up. I can't get a grip on that because normal people don't do that. We folks hold grudges and stuff. We don't forgive as easily. I guess the love that God has for us is different than the love we have for each other. I don't understand why.

I remember in Sunday school that we are to love each other as God loves us (John 15:12). My Sunday school teacher said "that love covers a multitude of sins."

> Above all things have intense and unfailing love for one another, for love covers a multitude of sins [forgives and disregards the offenses of others].
>
> 1 Peter 4:8 (AMP)

I think that's why Jesus' love is so forgiving because when we do bad things, his love forgives our offenses toward him. It was hard for me to forgive Brian and Lisa. I had to really work at letting their offenses towards me go. I hope one day I can be like Jesus and let things go and forgive people easily like he does.

I caught up with Theresa, my BFF. I told her what happened at the party during lunch period. I also apologized that she didn't get an invite and that I went without her. I told her she didn't miss a thing. She was forgiving. It was so cool. She doesn't care about the *popular crowd* as much as I do. She pretty much stays away from them and they for some reason stay away from her.

I have a ton of homework tonight and I have dance ministry practice. Theresa and I carpool to dance practice. It seems like we are back being best friends again. I think going to the party drove a separation between us, but it didn't last long. Theresa and I were soon giggling and having fun again.

I told Theresa about getting born-again the other day in Ms. Ruthie's office. It was so awesome. I shared that I had confessed all the things I did to God and he forgave me on the spot. I just had to come to him and speak. She said that she got saved at the Youth Explosion last summer. She did however felt she needed to pray to God about a few things that she has been thinking and doing. But she just blew it off. I told her that she shouldn't blow it off especially when God wants to bless her and do good things in her life. Theresa is pretty passive about God. It seems like she is just going through the motions because her family goes to church.

"You know, Nicolette; I guess I've been pretty laid back about my relationship with God. Since I got saved, I've not been working on it like I should."

"Well maybe if you start new and fresh, it will get better?"

"I guess I couldn't hurt to start over."

"You know I heard that God is the God of second, thirds, and fiftieth chances," I said. "He doesn't hold anything against us; but we have to have a heart to repent."

"What's the repent thing again?"

"That's when we turn completely from our sin and never to do it again. It's like in math class when we learn 180 degrees. We're turning 180 degrees away from where we are, or basically in the opposite direction, which basically means don't do that sin again."

"Oh I see."

"Hey, Theresa, do you wanna repent and turn from where you are to the direction facing God?"

"Sure I guess I can do that."

"Now, Theresa, you gotta be serious about it. You have to put effort into it not just do it just because."

"Maybe I should think about it first."

"But what if it's too late and you get hit by a car or in an accident and you die and you didn't commit to Jesus. Then you're going to leave me here wondering if you made it to heaven. Don't put me through that, Theresa."

We laughed. She said, "I don't think it's about you, Nicolette. I have to do it myself."

"Yep, you're right."

"Weird stuff has been happening all over the nation with kids getting killed and stuff. I don't wanna die and not be right with God."

"It's scary, isn't it?"

"I'm afraid to die, but I'm more afraid of not going to heaven. I hear it's a beautiful place and I can eat all I want and not gain weight, I can still be young and I can stay up as late as I want."

"For sure, and you can see Jesus and all the disciples when you get there,"

"I can see my grandma, too. I really miss her. She died a few years ago."

"I remember that. She was a saint."

"Yep, she was an elder, and gave to missionaries because she couldn't go overseas because of her cataracts and diabetes. She helped in the community with fundraisers for cancer. It's weird that cancer took her life."

"I know, Theresa. But I remember when she was sick and we went to see her in the nursing home…remember what she said?" I asked.

"Yes, she said to stay close to God and obey his word. She was smiling as if she couldn't wait to see him. She was sure she was going to heaven," said Theresa.

"Yeah, I think she was ready to go."

"Well let's do this prayer. I made up my mind that I don't want to miss heaven. I want to stay close to God like my grandma told me. I should make an effort to try to know him and his commands; to obey them."

"Awesome, Theresa, I have that card from our Youth Explosion. Remember that?"

"Yep, I remember. I don't know where mine went."

"I still have it in my Bible. I use it as a bookmark."

"Can you pass it to me at school tomorrow?"

"Better yet, I'll give it to you tonight before my mom drops you off at home. I'll have her stop by the house so I can grab it."

"Okay, that would be great. Thank you."

"Promise me, Theresa, that you'll give your life to Jesus tonight."

"Okay, I promise. I know it's time that I get serious. There's a lot of crazy people out there stealing kids and killing them. I want God to protect me."

"He will. I think his word says so."

> I do not ask that You will take them out of the world, but that You will keep and protect them from the evil one.

John 17:15 (AMP)

I was so excited for Theresa. I think she is going to go for it with God. I watched her tonight. She danced a little more forceful. I saw that she was really giving her all. We finished sweaty and tired. I felt a renewed joy and so did Theresa. I think that was the worship we needed to get some stuff off of us. We danced to Kirk Franklin's "Now Behold the Lamb."

My mom let me stop by the house to get the salvation card out of my Bible to pass to Theresa, and then we took

Theresa home. She was on fire. I went home with a bunch of homework to do and I then went to bed.

Theresa went up to her room and turned on her MP3 player. Candice Glover's song "I am Beautiful" was playing. Before Theresa got out of her sweaty clothes from dance practice, she closed the door of her bedroom and kneeled down and prayed the salvation prayer. She had tears in her eyes and she felt her grandma would have been proud of her. She just stayed there in the moment for a couple of more tracks of Candice's song.

I saw Theresa in church Sunday morning; she looked different. It was as if a dark cloud was lifted from her. Not that she had darkness about her, but she looked brighter. I smiled and gave her a hug. I knew she said the salvation prayer.

"How did it go for you, Theresa?"

"It was awesome. I want to thank you for sharing with me. I don't think I would have done it if you didn't share your thoughts and card with me."

"Wow cool, no problem."

"It felt good, it felt right, I confessed to the Lord my sins. I thought it would be better to do that and I felt comfortable since I was alone in my room. I just laid there for a bit and got up showered and went to bed."

"So cool, I'm so happy for you," I said. "You'll see, Theresa, things are going to change for the better in your life."

Theresa's life wasn't in a shambles, but she had been through some tough times with her father getting laid off, her grandmother dying, and her big brother getting arrested for drug possession. Well it was Tuesday again and I was back with Ms. Ruthie. I had some good news to share with her about Theresa.

"Hey, Ms. Ruthie, how are you?"

"Well, Nicolette, you're very excited today. Hello, how are you doing? I think I'd like some of that energy you have!"

"Guess what. I made things right with my BFF Theresa and after dance practice, she gave her life to Christ."

"Really, that's wonderful!"

"Yep I gave her my salvation card from last summer's Youth Explosion. She said that she gave her life over to Christ at the Explosion, but she felt that she wasn't working on her relationship with Jesus so she wanted to try again and make some changes."

"Oh that's so awesome, Nicolette. You see you're spreading the love of Christ. You're becoming quite the evangelist!"

"Wow, I didn't think about that."

"Yes, that's what happens when you dedicate your life to Christ, you become part of his team and he'll be with you as you walk out his will for your life."

> Jesus came and told his disciples, "I have been given all authority in heaven and on earth. Therefore, go and make disciples of all the nations, baptizing them in the

name of the Father and the Son and the Holy Spirit.
Teach these new disciples to obey all the commands
I have given you. And be sure of this: I am with you
always, even to the end of the age."

Matthew 28:18–20 (NLT)

"That's one of his commandments isn't it, Ms. Ruthie?"
I asked.

"Yes that's one of them. I see you've already embraced
it. That's great, and I know that God's pleased with you.
Keep it up, Nicolette. You may even express it in your
dance ministry as well. There are different ways that God
expresses his love, grace, and mercy. There are different ways
that people receive salvation. There's never a set pattern. It's
between that person and God."

"Yep, I see that because Theresa did it differently. She
gave her life to Christ behind her closed bedroom door on
her knees."

"That's perfectly fine, too. What matters is the heart
of the person and their confession with their mouth. They
can be anywhere in the world, in the jungle, hotel room,
prison, hospital, youth camp, in a boat on the ocean, in a
snowstorm on top of a mountain, anywhere. In all those
places, God is there receiving the person into his family,
washing them clean by the blood he spilled on Calvary."

"That's so cool."

"Yes, it's not difficult to come to Christ and it really
doesn't matter what condition or state you're in. You can

be drunk, sick, depressed, oppressed, diagnosed insane, or suicidal. It doesn't matter to Jesus. He takes you just the way you are. He'll clean you up and set you free."

"You know what stuck out when Theresa shared her salvation story with me? She said that she was laid back in her relationship with God."

"Oh you mean that she was pretty passive about it. She really wasn't putting her all in it."

"Yeah, that's right. How can she change that, Ms. Ruthie?"

"Well after we give our lives to Christ, or get born-again, or another word for it is *saved*, we go through a process called *sanctification*. One thing in our hearts that allows the sanctification process to be fruitful in our lives is we have a fear of the Lord."

"You mean we're afraid of what God will do to us when we screw up?

"No, let me give you the definition of the *fear* I'm talking about. According to Merriam-Webster dictionary, fear is to have a reverential awe of God, which is showing and having a lot of respect, and the motivation for surrender to him.[1] For those who have not given their lives over to Christ, then fear to them is fearful of judgment."

"Oh yeah, because Theresa and I were talking about missing heaven if there's an accident and we die without giving our lives to Christ and repenting."

"But since you and Theresa are believers and have accepted salvation of Christ then the fear of God motivates you to continually surrender yourself, your emotions, your sins, and your will over to his. Therefore, you're in a position to get all that he is and are obedient to his ways even with his discipline. In this choice of fearing God, you escape the fear of judgment and eternal separation from him. Do you understand?"

"Yes, the fear of God means we respect him and his Word so much that it dominates in our lives. When we fear God we get the best."

"Allow me to share a few words of wisdom with you. Let's turn to the book of Psalms and then to Proverbs and see what it means to fear God."

> Fear the Lord, you his godly people, for those who fear him will have all they need.
>
> Psalms 34:9 (NLT)

> For his unfailing love toward those who fear him is as great as the height of the heavens above the earth. He has removed our sins as far from us as the east is from the west. The Lord is like a father to his children, tender and compassionate to those who fear him.
>
> Psalms 103:11–13 (NLT)

> All you who fear the Lord, trust the Lord! He is your helper and your shield.
>
> Psalms 115:11 (NLT)

Fear of the Lord is the foundation of true wisdom. All who obey his commandments will grow in wisdom. Praise him forever!

Psalms 111:10 (NLT)

"Do you see the benefits of fearing the Lord? Do you have any question on these Scriptures?"

"No, I get it."

"There are quite a number of Scriptures on fear of the Lord and on wisdom. I don't want to overwhelm you, just give you a sense of what it means to fear God. So the last Scripture says 'fear of the Lord is the foundation of wisdom, which means that fearing God is the wisest thing you could do. Let's look at what the Book of Proverbs says.'"

Fear of the Lord is the foundation of true knowledge, but fools despise wisdom and discipline.

Proverbs 1:7 (NLT)

For wisdom will enter your heart, and knowledge will fill you with joy.

Proverbs 2:10 (NLT)

Get wisdom; develop good judgment. Don't forget my words or turn away from them.

Proverbs 4:5 (NLT)

> In the same way, wisdom is sweet to your soul.
> If you find it, you will have a bright future, and your
> hopes will not be cut short.

Proverbs 24:14 (NLT)

"How do I get wisdom?" I replied.

"You get wisdom by asking God for it."

"That's it?"

"Ask and believe you have received it," she replied. "Once I asked for wisdom, Nicolette, you won't believe the revelation and downloads I got from God on many different occasions and decisions in my life.

"I look back on those decisions without a doubt or regret because the wisdom of God was an integral part of them.

"Okay, let's look at these Scriptures briefly. So when you fear the Lord, he's unfailing love toward you provides all your needs. He helps you in your trouble; he's your shield, divine protection. The Bible says that when you fear the Lord, you're on the right path of true wisdom; wisdom of God. His wisdom is good knowledge, you can make the right choices and judgments, and it promises a bright future and hope. Why? Because when you fear the Lord, you make the decision to follow and hold fast to his words; thus, you have hope, peace, sweetest of your soul, and a wonderful future."

"Wow, very cool. I just have to hold onto Jesus's words and obey them. That means I have to repent of some stuff I do and think."

"Yes, Nicolette, there's another Scripture that says that in fearing the Lord you trust him. You can trust him in every area of your life because he's faithful.

"I remember it took many years for me to trust God. I'd always have my plan and try to put God in it. I didn't trust the plan that God had for me because I was so hurt from my past. I had sinned, and others have sinned against me. I had a double whammy of pain and hurt from my own sin and from the sins against me. But God had to take me through some seasons to show himself to me and in me. He had to take me through some things in my life where I had to get humble for my sins and also healing from the pain by others. As I went through these seasons in my life, I learned to trust God more and more. I learned to let go, to repent, forgive, to be grateful, and to receive. I was very much a giver, but not good at receiving. So God had to show me how to receive."

"Oh man. I bet it was tough huh?"

"Yes it was, but the Lord was patient with me and compassionate. He loved me through it and never left me in those tough times. The Holy Spirit guided and taught me Scriptures on trusting God, not to worry, not to be discouraged, and not to give up on Jesus.

"I'm telling you this because I don't want you to go through the long hard route like I did," she said. "It's good that you learn this now in your life. You see I learned these Scriptures and others in my forties; a lot had transpired and I was set in my ways of doing things. It was challenging to come to God like a child."

"Thanks, Ms. Ruthie, I appreciate you sharing," I said. "I think the best thing for me to do is to ask God for wisdom and keep on fearing him. I think when I ask him for help like that, he would help in times where I'm not feeling good about myself or my situation."

"Yes he'll be there for you faithfully, every time!" she said. "Keep me posted on how it's going for you. God will show up just in time, just ask."

"Our time today is up. I hope this was helpful to you."

"Oh yes it sure was," I replied.

"I want you to go home and meditate on these fear and wisdom Scriptures. See if you can find others on the same topics and bring them back and we can discuss. You can use a concordance to help you," she said.

"Okay, I'll do that. My mom has a Bible concordance on the bookshelf. See ya, Ms. Ruthie."

"Have a great week and I'll see you next time. Great job with your friend Theresa!"

Your Turn

After you prayed the prayer of salvation and received Jesus as your Lord and Savior, were you excited to tell someone?

1. If so, what did you share with them?

2. How did they respond to your testimony? If they didn't respond the way you have hoped, don't be discouraged, you planted a seed in them; something for them to think about. Just pray for them and allow God to work in their lives.

3. Find Scriptures about the "the fear of God" and "wisdom." What other benefits are there when you seek God's wisdom?

What Pedicure?

It was Saturday evening and my mom dropped Theresa and I off at the roller-skating rink. It was Christian night. I love songs from Casting Crowns, Third Day, Mary Mary, and Kirk Franklin. Theresa and I were having a blast. We were cool with Christ and I knew he was cool with us. We both looked great in our outfits and we didn't care what anyone said; we were gorgeous. The DJ did a great job spinning the CDs. We fell down a bunch of times. I think we even tripped up people while we were trying to get up.

The pizza at the rink is Tops. I always get the pepperoni. Theresa likes their extra cheese. As we were eating our pizza, Kevin, Kim, and Sharon stopped by. They joined us and told us more details about getting in trouble with their parents from that party a couple of weeks ago. I was surprised to see them there. I'd thought they would be grounded for life.

We saw Lisa on the rink floor. She was skating with David. I would say she was throwing herself at him. I didn't care. I had moved past them two. I felt pretty good when I saw them both. I'm sure I moved forward in forgiving.

Kevin asked Theresa to skate. We all looked at each other and grinned. Theresa rolled her eyes and headed to the skate floor with Kevin. They were playing a slow song, "How Beautiful" by Twila Paris. Kevin is a pretty good skater. He can skate backwards and forwards. He held Theresa by her waist and everything. She was totally blushing, but was cool about it.

David and Lisa came around the turn and almost tripped up Theresa as they sailed past her and Kevin. Kevin made sure she didn't fall. That was so cool. Lisa and David didn't even acknowledge their interference and kept skating like nothing happened. My goodness how can they be so coy. I think they need Jesus. I looked around the rink and I said Jesus please help my friends that don't know you. I said out loud "Jesus come and save them." Sharon and Kim just looked at me weird.

"What are you talking about?" asked Sharon.

"Oh I was just praying for some folks that's all," I replied.

"Why are you praying?" asked Kim.

"Oh, it was just a quick prayer that Jesus would come into the lives of the kids here and touch 'em that's all," I replied.

"Has Jesus touched you, Nicolette?" Kim asked.

"He has and it was awesome," I replied.

"How did he do that?" Sharon asked.

"I prayed and he answered my prayer. I got born-again and he has made me new. He touched me, I felt it on the inside," I replied.

"Wow, interesting. I didn't think he could touch people," said Kim.

"Yeah, it brings you to tears sometimes, but it's not a sad tear but a happy one," I replied. "Have you guys received salvation from the Lord?" I asked.

"Yep at the Youth Explosion last summer, remember?" said Sharon.

"Oh yeah, I remember."

"Did you feel Jesus's presence?" I asked.

"No, I felt warm inside and I felt free to do anything. I praised him hard. It was liberating," said Sharon.

"Wow, then he has touched you. I think he does things different for different people," I said.

"I guess so, I really didn't think about the fact that he touched me, but how I was feeling, you know?" Sharon said.

"Yeah, I know," I replied.

"For me, I was crying too because I had the godly sorrow for my sins that Pastor Chris was preaching about," said Kim. "I felt free not heavy from guilt."

"That is so cool you picked up on that," I replied.

Theresa and Kevin came back to the table. Theresa complained her feet were hurting. Matter of fact mine were, too. I think I was getting a blister on the bottom of my foot. I didn't wear thick socks, like I usually do. My big toe was rubbing against my skate. Perhaps this was evidence of another growth spurt my mom has been talking about since I was little.

We all went out on the skating rink floor for the last two songs even though our feet were hurting. Everyone was skating crazy until the lights came on and they ushered us off the floor to return our skates and go home. Theresa and I said "good-bye" to the gang and met my mom out front.

"Did you have a good time, girls?" mom asked.

"We did, we had so much fun," I replied. "We saw some of our friends from dance ministry there too."

"That's good," she said.

"I think we have some bumps and bruises from falling down. Lisa and David was their, Mom," I said.

"How did you respond to them?"

"I didn't have a problem with them at all. They were skating the slow song together while we were eating."

"Well it's good that you can move on from offenses and hurt and still have forgiveness toward them, Nicolette. I'm proud of you."

"It was a long journey, Mom, but thanks. I realized that I wanted to be right with Jesus. I think that helped my getting over it."

I'm glad we didn't have a dance presentation in church the next morning. I was tired, and my feet were killing me.

I finished my homework Sunday afternoon. I was bored. There was nothing on cable TV. I called Theresa and gabbed on the phone for a while. I was teasing her about her skate dance with Kevin. She was laughing. She was pretty mad about what Lisa and David's interference when they skated by them. Theresa said her foot tripped from under her and she lost her balance, but Kevin grabbed her underneath her arms, like directly in her arm pits and keep her from falling. She said good thing she had deodorant on and wasn't too sweaty from skating. We laughed so hard. I shared with Theresa that she had to forgive Lisa and David, even though they didn't say sorry for what they have done. She was in agreement. She said that she will work on it since she was making a fresh start with her relationship with Jesus.

Monday night came around and I didn't have much homework. I was bored so I decided to look in my mom's concordance and look up some Scriptures about wisdom and the fear of God that Ms. Ruthie gave me for homework. I looked back on the Scripture she shared with me not to repeat those.

I like that King Solomon guy. He was pretty wise. I bet if he were here, he would hold a student conference and tell us about his life and the wisdom that God blessed him with. He speaks so frankly. I bet he was cool to hang out with. His dad, oh my gosh, his dad was King David. That meant that Solomon was a prince who later became king.

I found a few Scriptures that were easy for me to understand. Ms. Ruthie was right about asking God for wisdom, he won't get mad when you ask for it. Boy when I get the wisdom of God, my face will be light and soft: I won't be looking mean or anything. I know why, because with God's wisdom I will be successful.

I'll be successful and have riches and a long life if I start on the right path with God and not choose the wrong path. I think the kids at the party were taking the wrong path. But, there is still opportunity for them to get on the right path with Jesus. I can believe it. No one can't deny God's word; it so simple.

> If you need wisdom, ask our generous God, and he will give it to you. He will not rebuke you for asking.
>
> James 1:5 (NLT)

> How wonderful to be wise, to analyze and interpret things. Wisdom lights up a person's face, softening its harshness.
>
> Ecclesiastes 8:1 (NLT)

> Using a dull ax requires great strength, so sharpen the blade. That's the value of wisdom; it helps you succeed.
>
> Ecclesiastes 10:10 (NLT)

> Those who follow the right path fear the Lord; those who take the wrong path despise him.
>
> Proverbs 14:2 (NLT)

> True humility and fear of the Lord lead to riches, honor, and long life.
>
> Proverbs 22:4 (NLT)

> Don't envy sinners, but always continue to fear the
> Lord.
>
> Proverbs 23:17 (NLT)

Tuesday came around again. I shared the Scriptures I found on *fear of God* and *wisdom* with Ms. Ruthie. She enjoyed them and said I did a great job in finding them on my own. I told Ms. Ruthie about our fun at the skating rink. I shared that Lisa and David almost tripped up Theresa and Kevin while they were skating.

"Did Theresa fall?" asked Ms. Ruthie.

"No, Kevin had a good hold on her," I replied.

"God is like that to you know."

"What do you mean?"

"He keeps our feet from slipping or stumbling."

"So God holds us up under our armpits like Kevin did with Theresa?"

"Yes I believe he does in many ways."

> You have made a wide path for my feet to keep them
> from slipping.
>
> Psalm 18:36 (NLT)

> Our lives are in his hands, and he keeps our feet from
> stumbling.
>
> Psalm 66:9 (NLT)

"Oh wow and I just found that Scripture that says fearing the Lord puts us on a right path. So if we chose and follow his path, then he won't let us stumble and fall?" I asked.

"What loving father would let their children fall unless his children are disobedient and correction is needed? We all learn from our mistakes and failures, they make us stronger." she said.

"It sounds so simple."

"It's easy. But sometimes when we're in the midst of trouble, turmoil, or feeding the desires of our flesh, then it's a hard decision to make. Because what we want may not be what God wants for us. But God is patient for us to repent (Joel 2:13)," she said.

> Don't tear your clothing in your grief, but tear your hearts instead. Return to the Lord your God, for he is merciful and compassionate, slow to get angry and filled with unfailing love. He is eager to relent and not punish.
>
> Joel 2:13 (NLT)

"Oh you know what that sounds like, Ms. Ruthie? It sounds like Kim's dad."

"How so?" she asked.

"Kim's dad gave his testimony about his struggle with alcohol. He said it was only God that brought him through it. But he said it was hard to turn from alcohol and clean himself up because he wanted to keep drinking, but a part of him wanted to stop to keep his marriage and family together. The pastor and elders got with him and helped him through his process. He said it took a lot of prayer. He has been sober for five years now."

"Well that's a wonderful testimony. I love to hear how God works in people's lives! God's love intervened in his life and kept his foot from slipping; kept him from holding on, and even turning back to the bottle. God didn't punish him but loved him despite his problem. Kim's dad changed his heart and chose the right path, and God did the rest."

"That's amazing."

"There are so many people that God has freed from drugs, alcohol, abuse, and even death. He gets all the glory. He has even chosen these folks to be his ministers of the Gospel. Now that they have been freed they completely understand the addiction and how God can free them from it. They make good messengers of the Gospel for those who need help with such addictions.

"Let's look at one more scripture, then we will dismiss."

> How beautiful on the mountains are the feet of the messenger who brings good news, the good news of peace and salvation, the news that the God of Israel reigns!
>
> Isaiah 52:7 (NLT)

"Okay, if the messenger is a minister and he or she is running through the mountains, shouldn't their feet be dirty and filthy?" I asked.

"Well we'd think so, but it's more symbolic. It says that how beautiful is the messenger's coming; it's attractive, it's delightful, and is honored. It's his haste, and his running, his feet that are beautiful. He hastily brings a message of good things, of peace; which is reconciliation with God. There were two kinds of messengers back in those days; those who had a good report and those who had an evil report. Those running with a good report, like the Gospel looked beautiful in the eyes of the weary, oppressed, and the afflicted," she explained.

"It sounds like the messenger was a sight for sore eyes," I replied.

"That's right. Those who proclaim the message of the Gospel brings joy to their hearers. So you see, Nicolette, you're beautiful because you brought the good news to Theresa. She listened and acted upon it."

"I know, and she looked different. Her face was lighter or something. She was touched. I didn't run to her like the Scripture says here."

"Yes but you didn't delay, you acted in haste because you wanted her to experience the goodness of God as you did. Don't think that you're ugly. You're sharing the Gospel to others. You're beautiful because you carry God within in you. You're his messenger. We all are messengers. That's how we build God's kingdom."

"I get it. I was so excited; I didn't keep it to myself and shared it immediately so she could have more of God in her life."

"That's right, you got it!" she said. "It's like Christmas morning and you open your gifts. You're excited and immediately tell someone about it."

"I really didn't think I was doing that."

"That's the Holy Spirit working inside you and using you to touch others. So keep doing what you're doing,"

"This is so cool. I really enjoyed this. I'll see ya, Ms. Ruthie."

"Have a great week and I'll see you next time."

Your Turn

Nicolette and many others are messengers of the Gospel. It doesn't matter how old you are or what talents and gifts you do or don't have. God will use you to help and show himself to others. You are beautiful in the eyes to those who listen to your testimony of your salvation.

I challenge you to share your faith, and your testimony with a friend or relative. Tell them about the special gift of God's grace and mercy through his son Jesus Christ. Share like you do on Christmas morning when you opened your presents and you let everyone know what you got.

I Love Me Some Me

My sessions with Ms. Ruthie are finishing up before Christmas. I'll meet with her again after the New Year. We met again the following Tuesday and she gave me a different assignment.

"Hello, Ms. Ruthie."

"Hello, Nicolette, how was your week?"

"It was pretty good, no drama."

"How are you feeling about yourself since we have studied some Scriptures together over these past weeks?"

"I'm feeling a lot better about myself. A lot has happened. I know that Jesus loves me and he wants the best for me and that I can come to him and talk with him. I know that I'm different than most of the kids and school, Lisa and David, but I'm okay with being different. I think those Scriptures and the Holy Spirit help me realize that I'm special no matter my shape or size," I said. "I know of a girl at school that's in a wheelchair. I felt sorry for her because she can't do the things we can do. But you know what she's special to God, too."

"She's special to God, your right."

"I see that she sits alone a lot and some kids sneak up behind her and push her wheelchair without her permission. I remember one boy sneaked up behind her outside in the school courtyard and he flipped over her because her brakes were on. That was funny. I even saw her laugh. The boy had a good-sized bump on his head that day. He never did it again. That'll teach him. I think I'm going to invite her to eat lunch with us. I felt bad that I haven't asked her before."

"That would be awfully nice, Nicolette."

"Perhaps you can talk to her about Jesus. I know that God has a plan for her despite her disabilities."

"Yes I think I will," I said. "I've seen a lot of quadriplegics do great things. They win sports competitions, spelling bees; even help those who are less fortunate than themselves."

"I like to give honor to those soldiers that have given their lives for our country. Some of them come back from war with missing limbs, disfigured faces, and nightmare beyond reason. They were brave and to me they are heroes. Everyone one of those soldiers belongs to Christ. They counted the cost to fight for our freedom. We do the same with our faith. Sometimes it's a fight or struggle to get and keep our freedom in Christ Jesus, but we were bought for a price."

> But now [in spite of past judgments for Israel's sins], thus says the Lord, He Who created you, O Jacob, and He Who formed you, O Israel: Fear not, for I have redeemed you [ransomed you by paying a price

instead of leaving you captives]; I have called you by your name; you are Mine.

Isaiah 43:1 (NLT)

Endure suffering along with me, as a good soldier of Christ Jesus. Soldiers don't get tied up in the affairs of civilian life, for then they cannot please the officer who enlisted them. And athletes cannot win the prize unless they follow the rules. And hardworking farmers should be the first to enjoy the fruit of their labor. Think about what I am saying. The Lord will help you understand all these things.

2 Timothy 2:3–7 (NLT)

"I'd pray for our soldiers to come home. But as their time in war tarried, I prayed that the angels of protection would be around them in every second of their mission," she said.

"Nicolette, I'm proud that you're feeling good about your self-image and that you're specially made by God in his own image (Genesis 1:27). I want you to make a collage of some things that you can look back on in case you may have those yucky feelings again. I want you to build a collage with some beautiful things or words from different magazines to encourage you whenever you're feeling blue about yourself. Here are some words that may help you."

Ms. Ruthie went to her whiteboard in her office and wrote down some words that could be included in my collage. She wrote "Accept yourself," "Be True," "Love," "Believe," and "Thankful."

"I have some magazines from my beautician that you can take home and cut up for your collage. She was throwing them out. These words I listed will help you. Be creative. This is for you. If you have some favorite Scriptures, you can print them out and glue them on your poster. This is an expression of you, Nicolette, okay?"

"Okay, that sounds good."

I flipped through some of the magazines she gave me.

"Ms. Ruthie, these magazines are the kind that make you want to look like the model."

"What do you mean?"

"These magazines have skinny girls in them with a ton of makeup in best clothes. Their thighs don't even touch. It makes you want what they have and be like them."

"Oh I see. Well you can cut it up because you know better than try to be like them. Just be who God made you to be."

"Okay cool."

"Now I want you to think about these questions written here while you're building your collage."

She gave me a sheet of paper with three questions on them.

1. Read John 3:16 (AMP). If God loves you so much to give his son for an eternal relationship with you, why do you feel worthless? You are worthy of his love.

2. Read Ephesians 1:4–8 (NLT). In his love, God chose us and sees no fault in us by the blood of Jesus then why can't you love yourself?

3. Read Psalm 139:13–15 (NLT). The Lord made you wonderfully and skillfully. He knows you inside and out. Why don't you look upon yourself as a beautiful, marvelous workmanship of his hands?

I put the magazines and the question sheet in my book bag and grabbed the poster board and went home to start my project. I was excited to start. I didn't have much homework that night. I turned on my favorite CD, *Fresh* by Tye Tribbett. I dug through my desk drawers and found some glue. I spread the magazines on the floor and started flipping through them. I cut out words like "Beauty," "Love," and "Accept." I didn't find "believe" and "thankful" so I made them with individual letters cut out. I need some Scriptures on my poster board. I went downstairs and asked my mom if I could get online and print some out. She was cool with that. I found some Scriptures on my own when I was looking up "fear of God" and "wisdom" in the concordance. I like new things so I like this Scripture that says that I'm new in Christ Jesus.

> This means that anyone who belongs to Christ has become a new person. The old life is gone; a new life has begun!
>
> 2 Corinthians 5:17 (NLT)

Here is a couple more.

> I can do all things through Christ who strengthens me.
>
> Philippians 4:13 (NKJV)

> What shall we say about such wonderful things as these? If God is for us, who can ever be against us?
>
> Romans 8:31 (NLT)

I shortened the Scriptures a bit and cut out the letters for each word.

Such as "God is for me, who can be against me," "I can do all things," "I'm made new." I added some pictures of pretty scenery, added some handbags I liked, some hearts, some music notes, I like music, so I added a couple of my favorite artists. I still have a lot more to do; only half of my board was covered.

I propped the poster board on my dresser against the wall. I stood back and checked it out. I thought about what these words and pictures mean to me. They will help me for sure. I was happy with it. I sat on my bed and read the worksheet that Ms. Ruthie gave me. I read the first question. I thought about if I ever felt worthless. I guess I do sometimes when I'm around people of authority like our pastor or school principal. I don't know why I feel that way they are just here to help. I don't think it's a matter of worthiness, but I feel like a second-rate citizen. I know

I shouldn't feel this way. This John 3:16 Scripture totally blows that thinking out the water, but God loved me enough to deny his own son for my salvation. I guess that means I was worth much to him.

Okay, the second question is Ephesians 1:4–8. Hmm I'm adopted in to the Lord's family through Jesus Christ. That's kinda cool. It's like someone who marries into a wealth family. I am in a family with good genes, much love, wealth, and wisdom. Who could possibly pass that up? Are you kidding me? I will do everything I can to stay in his family.

Okay the last question is Psalm 139:13–15. Ms. Ruthie I think shared this one with me. Not only am I adopted, but he made me way before Genesis chapter 1. He knows me inside and out and he still loves me. He will always love me. So I guess there is no reason for me to hate my boobs or hips. He loves what he made and I love God that made 'em.

I'm going to title my poster board, "I Love Me Some Me." No matter what someone says or does to hurt me, I'm still going to love myself because God will never stop loving me.

Your Turn

Nicolette went through the Scriptures and the corresponding thought questions. Think on these Scriptures for yourself. What's stopping you from feeling worthy, loving yourself, and accepting and loving your body?

For God so greatly loved and dearly prized the world that He [even] gave up His only begotten (unique) Son, so that whoever believes in (trusts in, clings to, relies on) Him shall not perish (come to destruction, be lost) but have eternal (everlasting) life.

John 3:16 (AMP)

Even before he made the world, God loved us and chose us in Christ to be holy and without fault in his eyes. God decided in advance to adopt us into his own family by bringing us to himself through Jesus Christ. This is what he wanted to do, and it gave him great pleasure. So we praise God for the glorious grace he has poured out on us who belong to his dear Son He is so rich in kindness and grace that he purchased our freedom with the blood of his Son and forgave our sins. He has showered his kindness on us, along with all wisdom and understanding.

Ephesians 1:4–8 (NLT)

You made all the delicate, inner parts of my body and knit me together in my mother's womb. Thank you for making me so wonderfully complex! Your workmanship is marvelous—how well I know it. You watched me as I was being formed in utter seclusion, as I was woven together in the dark of the womb.

Psalm 139:13–15 (NLT)

Who's In My Camp?

I felt pretty sick the next morning. I didn't know why. I looked at my poster and all the work I put into it. It wasn't complete yet, sometimes I rush through things. It's better to build it slow. I know one thing for sure, Jesus's name is on it. His letters I cut out are the biggest on the whole poster board.

I didn't feel like going to school, but I wanted to meet with Theresa and tell her about the poster board. I'll invite her over to show her the details. I'll know she will love it. I jumped up showered, dressed, and went off to school. Winter is coming. It's cold outside. The mornings and early evenings are dark. We have been practicing for the Christmas program at church. We have practice tonight and tomorrow night. I hope I don't have a lot of homework. I have a math exam tomorrow I'm not looking forward to.

I stepped off the bus into a puddle of cold rainwater. I had a headache, and I was sore from dance practice. I looked up to the sky and could have said something I would have regretted, but said to myself, "Jesus, help me today." Thank goodness I had an extra pair of socks in my locker. They were kinda smelly from gym, but I don't like my feet and socks being wet; especially all-day long. I was changing my socks when Theresa stopped over.

"Hey, Nic," she said, "You never would guess who asked me to the Christmas program dance at church?

"Who?"

"Kevin."

"Oh, wow really? That's great!"

"Do you really like him?"

"I guess, he's okay," she said. "I'm surprised that he wants to hang out with me. Why me? Is this some joke?"

"No, I don't believe it's a joke at all. He likes you. You're very pretty Theresa. It about time you start to see that in yourself."

"I don't know…whatever. I just want to get outta here and see the world, Nicolette. I want to travel and…oh I don't know what I want."

"Pray about it, Theresa. Pray about everything. I learned that from Ms. Ruthie. She said that God can help you in every area of your life, and he's with you everywhere you go."

"I know. You're right," she said. "I'll ask Jesus and he'll give me an answer. I believe he will."

"Are you going with someone?"

"To the dance?" I asked. "No, but I'll be there."

"I gotta go class, I'm late. See you at lunch."

"Yeah okay. Oh, Theresa. Let's invite Sarah over to eat with us today."

"Sarah that's in the wheelchair?"

"Yes. I want to befriend her; let's see where it goes."

"Okay, see you then."

"I was not feeling 100 percent, my head was bounding. I sat in four class periods daydreaming and thinking about what I wanted to do after high school. Theresa brought up a good point. I never thought about it seriously. I mean what I wanted to do after high school. I guess I better be praying about it. I really need help to see what is next in my life. I want to go to college. My mom always said that I would be going to college. She has been saving up for it. She says that companies are raising the bar in hiring. An applicant used to get a job with just a high school diploma, in her generation you need a bachelor's degree. Now many jobs expect a MBA or graduate degree.

I just don't know where and what I want to study for a career. Let's see now, what is it I like to do? I remember Ms. Ruthie said that she started off as an engineer, and then she ended up in ministry. That's a weird combination. The Lord works in mysterious ways. Boy, I bet she was making some bucks. I don't know why she left engineering. Ministry doesn't pay much at all. She must have been in a car accident and hit her head. I'll have to ask her later. It was lunchtime and Theresa and I asked Sarah over for lunch.

"Hey, Sarah, thank for joining us," I said. "We just want to be friends with you."

"Why?" she asked.

"Why not?" I replied. "Theresa and I like meeting new people and getting to know them."

"Okay cool, thanks for inviting me."

"Do you like it here?"

"I do sometimes," she replied. "I know I have to get my education; I want to be a counselor to kids. I want to help them get through tough stuff in their lives."

"Wow, that's great!" Theresa said.

"So you have to go to college and get a bachelor's degree?"

"I'd probably need to get both the bachelor and master's degree, at least," she replied.

"I'm happy for you, Sarah," I replied.

"Thanks, I want to help kids who have been through divorce, in tornadoes, and lost everything, including family members."

"Gee whiz, you've been through all that Sarah?" Theresa asked.

"Yes and I'm still here," she replied. "I get sad sometimes but I pray."

"Wow, you pray too? I asked.

"Yes, I pray to Jesus. If it wasn't for him we wouldn't be here. I was angry that the tornado hit our home and killed my stepdad, but we got help from some people who were helping with the cleanup. They gave us food, water, and a place to sleep and shower. They also prayed with us and listened to my mother cry and scream. I was in the hospital recovering from my injuries and got stuck in this wheelchair. Someone who belongs to the church paid my hospital bill," she replied. "We don't know who did it."

"My goodness, that was awfully nice of them to help you," I said.

"The cleanup crew connected us with a local pastor and we gave our lives to Christ," she said.

"You guys just moved here huh?"

"Yeah my mom decided not to rebuild, so my mom, two brothers, and I moved here closer to the city."

"So you're going to be like a messenger to the kids you're going to counsel, right?

"I don't know, I guess," she said. "I just want to help. I like talking about Jesus."

"That's awesome," I said. "Some people don't have a heart to help others especially after a loss like that. They live in their own world working for that dollar and for the man."

"You're going to be such a blessing to many kids, Sarah," Theresa said.

"This is so cool. We have a fellow believer to hang with us, Theresa," I said. "If you wanna hang with us, Sarah, we'd love to have you?"

"Okay. It's nice to be around people who don't call you Jesus freak, Bible thumper, or daddy's girl."

"You get that a lot?"

"Yeah sometimes," she said. "My mom says that's okay, when you live for Christ, there will be some persecution, trials, and trouble. It's hard sometimes, but I have friends, my brothers, and my mom to encourage me to hang in there with Jesus."

"That's good, you have us too, Sarah," I said.

"I saw you get teased the other day with the spaghetti on your shirt," said Sarah. "That took guts."

"Oh you saw that huh? Well it took something inside me not to hit Lisa for doing what she did," I replied.

"I guess you get persecuted too then?" she asked.

"I guess so." I said. "Ms. Ruthie, my mentor, has been helping me out a lot, of course my mom too. She gave me some wisdom and precautions about picking your battles. Most importantly we have been working on forgiveness. This forgiveness thing is so hard. I'm still working on it. I think I'm getting better with it because I don't want to do Lisa any harm or wish bad things on her. I used to though."

"My mom gave me a Scripture and helped me understand that there are a lot of Christians even today that are dying for their faith," said Sarah.

> Yes, and everyone who wants to live a godly life in Christ Jesus will suffer persecution.
>
> 2 Timothy 3:12 (NLT)

"Do you think that the tornado and what your family suffered was persecution?" Theresa asked.

"I don't know, but God showed up in our lives for some reason. I still don't understand the whole thing except that

God has a plan for me and he obviously isn't done with me. Besides we weren't going to church then like we are now. We didn't follow Jesus like we do now. We have a lot to be thankful for. We got a chance at salvation even though it was through hard times."

> God is our refuge and strength, always ready to help in times of trouble.
>
> Psalm 46:1 (NLT)

> Furthermore, because we are united with Christ, we have received an inheritance from God, for he chose us in advance, and he makes everything work out according to his plan.
>
> Ephesians 1:11 (NLT)

I wanted to sit and talk to Sarah some more. The bell rang for fifth period and we had to go to our next class. Boy she went through a lot of stuff. I feel bad for her, but at the same time I feel good that she is not going to let the tragedy her family faced discourage her for the rest of her life.

I sat in my classes the rest of the afternoon still contemplating my future. My headache disappeared. Sarah has definitely got her act together in what she wants to do. I don't think God takes everyone through tragedy to show them the way, but I believe that he will in any circumstance.

This is my last meeting with Ms. Ruthie before the Christmas break. Perhaps she can give me some pointers on what to do for college and beyond.

"Hello, Nicolette!" she said. "How are you doing?"

"Hey, Ms. Ruthie, I'm fine, how are you doing?"

"Very well, thank you. I have a form for you to complete. Pastor and the program director want to know how our mentoring sessions are going."

"I'm going to give you ten out of ten, Ms. Ruthie!"

"Oh thank you, Nicolette, but I want you to focus on anything that worked well and didn't work well. Please describe those occasions so we can improve. I'm going to step outside my office and let you do that."

After about five minutes, I peeped outside the door and motioned Ms. Ruthie to come back in. I gave her the form and was anxious to talk about college stuff.

"Ms. Ruthie, Theresa and I had lunch with Sarah the other day."

"How did that go?"

"It went well, she has been through a tornado, lost her stepdad, and she got stuck in a wheelchair from her injuries."

"Oh dear."

"But, Ms. Ruthie, check this out. Sarah wants to counsel kids who have been through tragedies like hers. She's also a Christian like us."

"That's wonderful."

"She knows what she wants to do. I don't know what to do after high school, Ms. Ruthie."

"Well, Nicolette, you have a tight relationship with God. You know that he'll answer your prayers. You also know that he'll guide you in the way you're to go. I challenge you to pray and seek him. Tell him the things you like to do and those things you don't like to do. Ask the Lord to reveal his plan in your life. You'll know, Nicolette. You'll know when he answers. You'll know the path for your future.

> I will instruct you and teach you in the way you should
> go; I will counsel you with my loving eye on you.
>
> Psalm 32:8 (NLT)

"I'll do that, Ms. Ruthie." I said.

"As we're nearing the end of our session today, Nicolette, I want to impress upon you to choose your friends wisely. Sarah sounds like a great friend, and I'm sure she blessed you with her testimony. But I want you learn this one thing; to choose your friends based on the word of God. It'll keep you from a broken heart and distress in life. So as you go off to high school, college, and even beyond college, chose your friends based on what the Lord says.

"I remember my mom said 'you choose your friends.' She told me that after I graduated college and off to graduate school. I'd say she was pretty late. I had been through hell with some boyfriends and even female friends in my life. It was hurtful, but nonetheless, I thanked my mom for sharing.

"A very important thing I really want you to put into practice with seeking God is in marriage. Please make sure that you seek and ask God whom you're to marry. He'll give the 'okay' if you have found the right one. The important thing is to be at peace when God tells you he's not the one no matter how you feel about him. God's protecting you even though you don't see it.

"You may think this is premature talking to you about marriage, but many girls dream of their wedding day and not carefully consider the person they'll spend the rest of their life with. Don't make the mistake of many. They marry the wrong person due to impatience or they think that they could change them. Their criteria for a husband may not necessarily meet God's criteria and standards. Thus they become unequally yoked. We'll talk more about this later, but I want to plant that seed in you today."

"Okay, Ms. Ruthie, I understand. So if I marry David, we have to be in agreement with God's ways and his commands right?"

"Yes, that's right, if that's not the case, run for the hills," she said. "It will save you a lot of heartache.

"So let me share a few more wisdom tips from God concerning friends. I remember you said that you didn't feel you fit in and that you're different than others. Well,

Nicolette, that's not a bad thing according to the word of God.

> Walk with the wise and become wise, for a companion of fools suffers harm.
>
> Proverbs 13:20 (NIV)

"Oooh those are some strong words," I said.

"Yes they are, take heed to them," she said. "Here's another one."

> Do not make friends with a hot-tempered person, do not associate with one easily angered, or you may learn their ways and get yourself ensnared.
>
> Proverbs 22:23–24 (NIV)

"I think Lisa has a bit of a temper in her. I see now that it would not be good to hang out with her and her temper," I said. "What does *ensnare* mean again?"

"It means to catch in trap from which there's not escape."[1]

"Yikes, *no escape*, that's scary. It sounds like prison."

> Do not be deceived: "Evil company corrupts good habits." Awake to righteousness, and do not sin; for some do not have the knowledge of God. I speak this to your shame.
>
> 1 Corinthians 15:33 (NKJV)

"This Scripture falls in line with unequally yoked. You don't compromise your faith in God with people who don't agree with your Godly principles. If they don't agree with the word of God, then cut them loose, or your righteousness in God will come to ruin.

"I found on several occasions the closer I got to God, the more my friends tugged at me to do the things they were doing; which was not of God. For example, hitting the bar scene and going out dancing in the clubs. I continued to go to the clubs after my salvation several times with my girlfriends, but I started not to like it anymore. I was wasting my money on alcohol and a sweaty dance with a guy that only wanted one thing, a one-night stand.

"I even had to let go of some Christian friends because they were not in agreement in giving up my career for the work of the Lord. I had lost a lot of friends along the way, but the Lord gave me new friends that encouraged me in the Word. They were mighty men and women of God that mentored me without any judgment; they were even there for me in the tough times to cry with me.

"But God was the one that rescued me. He's always first in any and every decision in my life. Remember, Nicolette, as you grow and mature in God. He'll always be the final say. If you get a prophetic word, check it with God. I got a prophetic word from someone who was twenty years younger than me. She definitely flowed in the Spirit, but I was cautious. I asked the Lord immediately 'does your prophet speak true, Lord?' The Lord answered 'yes,' and then I went home and wrote the prophecy down in my journal and waited for its manifestation."

"This is good stuff, Ms. Ruthie. I'm going to remember it," I replied.

"I'll write it down for you over the Christmas break and give it to you in our next session," she said.

"That sounds great, thank you!"

"Well I wish you and your mom a wonderful and blessed Christmas."

"Do you have plans, Ms. Ruthie?"

"I'm going to see you dance at the Christmas program and have been invited to Christmas Eve dinner. Christmas Day, my kids and grandkids will be coming over for dinner and gifts. What are you doing for Christmas?"

"That sounds good. I'll be having dinner with my mom and some friends from church. Then I'm going to hang out with Nicolette, Sarah, Kim, Kevin, and Sharon during the break," I replied.

"I wish you a very Merry Christmas, Nicolette. I'll see you the second week of January back here in my office."

"Okay, thank you, Ms. Ruthie. I got you a card."

"Oh thank you, Nicolette. I'm going to hang it on my door so I can see it. I have one for you and all my mentees."

"Okay I will. See ya."

"See ya."

Your Turn

Nicolette got some great wisdom regarding choosing good friends.

1. How are you with choosing your friends?

2. Are your friends getting you in trouble? Do you find that they are pressing you to do things that are against God's commands and your parent's rules?

3. Review these Scriptures and find out if you have someone in your life that may be leading you astray.

4. Ask God to help discern their characteristics if you are not clear and show you how to move on from the relationship.

> Walk with the wise and become wise, for a companion of fools suffers harm.
>
> Proverbs 13:20 (NIV)

> Do not make friends with a hot-tempered person, do not associate with one easily angered, or you may learn their ways and get yourself ensnared.
>
> Proverbs 22:23-24 (NIV)

> Do not be deceived: "Evil company corrupts good habits." Awake to righteousness, and do not sin; for some do not have the knowledge of God. I speak this to your shame.
>
> 1 Corinthians 15:33 (NKJV)

Notes

"My Beauty on the Outside"

1. "Low Self Esteem at Crisis Levels for Girls," Crosswalk.com http://www.crosswalk.com/family/parenting/low-self-esteem-at-crisis-levels-for-girls-11582765.html (assessed 2013).

"Wisdom From in High"

1. "fear." Merriam-Webster Incorporated, http://www.merriam-webster.com (assessed 2013).

"Who's in My Camp?"

1. "ensnare." Merriam-Webster Incorporated, http://www.merriam-webster.com (assessed 2013).